ESCAPE THIS BOOK!
TOMBS of EGYPT

You hold in your hands
the key to a world of mystery.

I have filled this action-packed adventure
with amazing facts about ancient Egypt. But
this is not a history book! To design the most
challenging and fun escapes, I've combined
real and made-up elements. Want to find
out more about the facts? Dig into my
Escapologist Files at the back of the book!

—The Master Escapologist

ESCAPE THIS BOOK!
TOMBS of EGYPT

BY BILL DOYLE
ILLUSTRATED BY SARAH SAX & YOU

Random House 🏠 New York

Text copyright © 2020 by Bill Doyle
Cover art and interior illustrations copyright © 2020 by Sarah Sax

All rights reserved. Published in the United States by Random House Children's Books, a division of Penguin Random House LLC, New York.

Random House and the colophon are registered trademarks of Penguin Random House LLC.

Visit us on the Web! rhcbooks.com

Educators and librarians, for a variety of teaching tools, visit us at RHTeachersLibrarians.com

Library of Congress Control Number: 2018956847

ISBN 978-0-525-64422-4 (trade)

Book design by Leslie Mechanic

Printed in the United States of America
10 9 8 7 6 5 4 3 2 1
First Edition

FOR ANN AND CURT . . .
AND THE THREE G BOYS
—B.D.

TO MOM, DAD, AND CARRIE—
FOR MAKING ART TOGETHER
—S.S.

Draw your face on this sphinx. The nose and fake pointy beard were lost many centuries ago. Put them back on!

This sphinx was carved about 4,500 years ago! With the body of a lion and the head of a pharaoh, it crouches by a tomb to protect the ruler in the afterlife.

FOLD HERE

When you're done drawing, fold this corner up toward you!

You are TRAPPED inside this book...
and this book is an ancient Egyptian TOMB!

In just a few pages, you'll be locked inside a burial chamber, or on the run from a mile-long snake, or in a chariot race across the desert.

Who am I? The world's greatest escapologist! I am in search of a helper for a very special mission. I will tell you more—including my location!—IF you prove yourself worthy by escaping this book.

While I am otherwise tied up, I've sent along my pet gopher, Amicus, to be my eyes and ears during your adventure. He is a master of disguise. (Not as talented as I am, of course!) You won't be able to see him until you draw him. I'll let you know when he's around so you can spot him!

Draw my gopher, Amicus, here!

I'm Amicus! When you're in a jam, that's where I am!

Your great escape will be even more exciting than you sphinx! Turn the page.

To survive, you'll need to *demolish*, *decide*, and *doodle* your way out of this book. A sharp pencil or a ballpoint pen will help you "pop" through pages when you have to doodle and demolish!

Practice your escapology with three quick challenges.

Demolish!
Quick Challenge #1

Don't be afraid to ruin perfect pages! Get ready to rip, fold, and scrunch when I tell you—every second counts!

In 1922, an archaeologist named Howard Carter discovered the entrance to the grave of King Tutankhamen. What did Carter see when he made a hole in the door of King Tut's tomb and stuck a candle inside?

Use your pencil or pen to poke a hole here. Now tear along the dotted line and fold over the flap toward you.

You'll need to make fast decisions—and solve my puzzles—as you pick your own escape path! My Escapologist Files at the back of the book are packed with helpful information. Flip to the files when I tell you, when you see this folder, or whenever you want!

Decide!
Quick Challenge #2

Have you heard of the mummy's curse? Many believe it can make you very sick—or even worse!

If you decide to find out more about the "curse" of King Tut before you enter an Egyptian tomb, flip to page 175.

PAGE 175

Or if you don't want to bother, take your chances and go to the next page!

"An astonishing sight . . . a solid wall of gold." That is what Carter first saw inside King Tut's tomb. Turn the page!

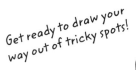

Get ready to draw your way out of tricky spots!

Doodle!
Quick Challenge #3

The Great Pyramid is the only remaining wonder of the Seven Wonders of the World. A monument and tomb for a pharaoh (ruler of ancient Egypt) named Khufu, it stood as the tallest building in the world for almost 4,000 years.

PAGE
175

What would you build so that people would remember your name forever? Draw it here!

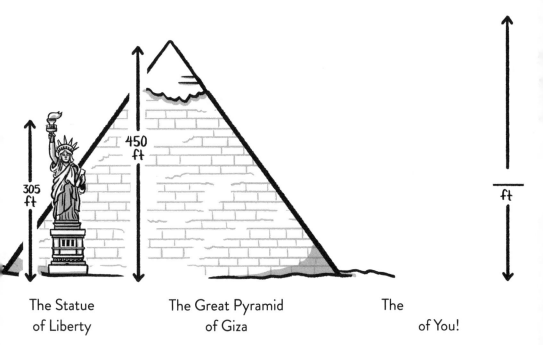

305 ft

450 ft

ft

The Statue
of Liberty

The Great Pyramid
of Giza

The
of You!

Almost 150 feet taller than the Statue of Liberty, the Great Pyramid is the largest of the 130 Egyptian pyramids discovered so far.

Turn the page.

Aces! You've got the basics down. Now let's see where in time you are!

The ancient Egyptian empire lasted for about 3,100 years. Its people were highly advanced (just like me!). Did you know the ancient Egyptians gave us the 24-hour day and the 365-day calendar? They invented pens, locks, keys, and even toothpaste, which was made of ox hooves, ashes, and burnt eggshells. Yum!

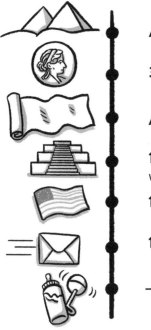

Around 3100 BCE—The ancient Egyptian empire begins.

30 BCE—The ancient Egyptian empire ends.

Around 100 CE—Paper is invented in China.

1325 CE—Aztecs start building the city of Tenochtitlán (in what is now central Mexico).

1776 CE—America declares its independence.

1971 CE—The first email is sent.

_____ CE—YOU are born!

↑
Write in the year
you were born.

You've arrived more than 5,000 years after the start of the ancient Egyptian empire. (Depending on the positions of the planets, you could travel to or from Mars about 6,600 times in that amount of time!)

Go to the next page.

Who will YOU be on this adventure?

You can choose three different paths through this book. Write your name in one of the blanks below and get started. I'll send you back here later to try the other paths!

PHARAOH

_____

Want to be the top ruler of ancient Egypt for a day? This path is based on one of history's greatest pharaohs, Hatshepsut. Your adventure will quickly take a turn to the unexpected—hold on tight!

Turn to page 8.

ARCHAEOLOGIST

_____

An archaeologist makes incredible discoveries—and you're no exception. You're about to uncover and enter an ancient hidden tomb . . . but can you get out?

Dig your way to page 76.

PYRAMID WORKER

_____

You're one of thousands of skilled workers who build the world's most amazing monuments. Will all that skill help you avoid being turned into a mummy?

Head to page 128.

Let your great escape begin!

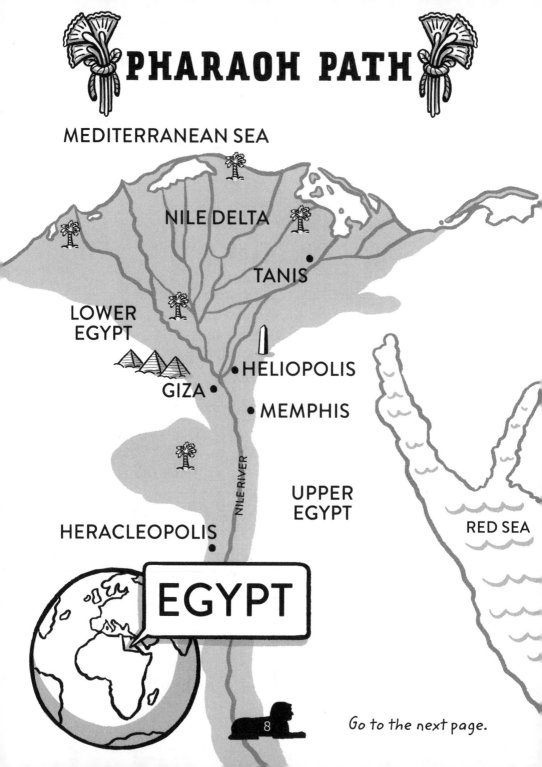

Go to the next page.

So you want to be in charge of ancient Egypt for a day? Okay, first prove you know how to dress like a pharaoh. If you don't flip to the back of the book, you're going to have to guess!

PAGE
176

Draw the crown of ancient Egypt on your head.

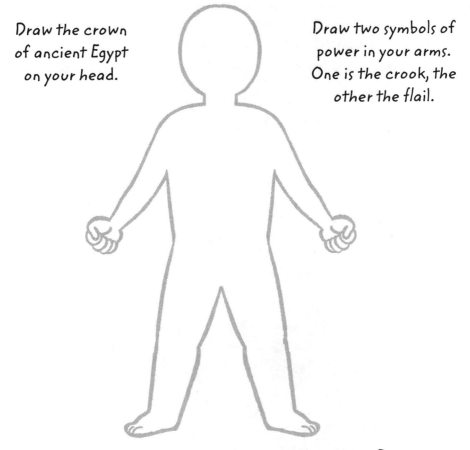

Draw two symbols of power in your arms. One is the crook, the other the flail.

Does your crown drawing include a chicken?

If yes, turn to page 27.
If no, go to page 10.

9

Hmm. Well, I guess your drawings are close enough.

Congratulations! It's 3,500 years ago and you're the top ruler in Egypt. Well, I should say, you're just minutes away from being named pharaoh—if you can complete your escape!

You're the oldest child of the current pharaoh, Tuthmosis I, and you're playing games in the royal garden with your nanny's four kids. Ineni, who's your age, is trying to teach the newest dance steps.

"No, no!" she tells you. "Do it like this!" You like Ineni, but she can be bossy at times.

(I certainly don't know anyone like that.
Now keep reading! HURRY UP!)

As Ineni kicks out one leg, she trips and falls. Her behind lands on a melon.

It's not proper for a divine being such as yourself to laugh at regular people, especially a friend. Ineni looks hurt when you giggle. But you can't help it!

Draw a melon squishing under Ineni.

Go to the next page.

Let's see if you can kick high, like Ineni! Put the tip of your pen here. Hold on to the top of the pen with any two fingers—but not your thumb. Now kick off by flicking your pen toward the targets. As you land on a flap, tear along the dotted lines and fold the flap over.

Sitting in the corner, a scribe clucks his tongue at your giggling. "Tsk, tsk," he says, and writes down your lack of kindness. You know he's working on a project for your dad about you. But you don't know what it is.

Scribes are historians who write down things that happen. When they sit cross-legged, they can use the stiff part of their kilts as portable writing desks.

Turn the page!

Kick higher!

Keep kicking!

You're not going to let the scribe ruin things.
You want to have fun.

"Let's try another game," you command. (You can do that . . . because you're royalty!)

Like all Egyptian kids, you love to race, wrestle, hit balls with palm branches—and play tug-of-war—but you don't use a rope! Instead, captains of the two teams lock hands, and their teams line up behind them, pulling them back. A team wins when it pulls everyone on the other team across a line.

Play tug-of-war! Draw friends or family you want on your team.

Fold down this corner when you're done drawing.

Did you draw three or more people on your team? If yes, turn to page 14. If no go to page 17.

"I won! I won!" you shout. Ineni and her friends look pretty upset as you laugh and do a happy dance. You spot the scribe scribbling down your reaction. *Who cares?* you think. You enjoy winning games . . . almost as much as you love your baboon that you can train to pick fruit. Your life as part of the royal family is jammed with perks—like amazing pets!

You LOVE all animals, but especially your baboon. Train him to pick the best fig on the tree! Here's how:

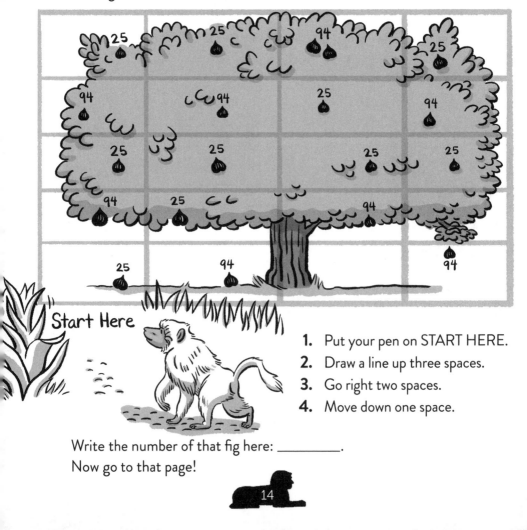

Start Here

1. Put your pen on START HERE.
2. Draw a line up three spaces.
3. Go right two spaces.
4. Move down one space.

Write the number of that fig here: _____.
Now go to that page!

Your heart is judged to be pure! Now you get to fly across the sky in the solar boat of Ra, the sun god!

Just as you're flying overhead, Apep springs into the air in front of you. He wants to stop Ra from taking the sun across the sky . . . and to eat you up, of course. Apep is trying to use his magical gaze to hypnotize Ra.

Um, quick! How will you escape the monstrous
Apep? Will you put him in a trance by reflecting
his hypnotic gaze? Or maybe flee through the air
in something faster than Ra's boat? What will you do?
Draw it here!

If you drew something
with a mirror or shield,
turn to page 68.

Did you draw a helicopter
or some other flying
machine? Turn to page 44.

Oh no! Is something wrong with your dad? You're so worried, your thoughts scatter.

Draw what you see in the numbered boxes in the correct parts of the grid below. Do you see your dad now?

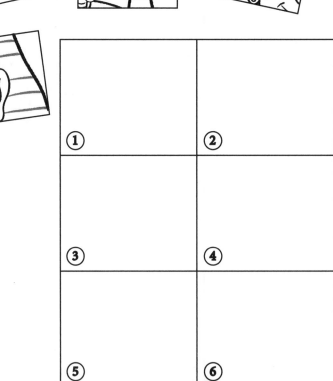

YOUR DAD, TUTHMOSIS I

If his earring is in his right ear, turn to page 162.

In his left ear? Go to page 65.

Ugh! You don't have enough people on your team. You get pulled so hard that you tumble over the bank of the nearby Nile River.

Luckily, you land on something before you actually hit the water.

*Did I say **luckily**? Um, I meant **unfortunately.** That thing you landed on? It's a hungry crocodile.*

END

Please don't feed the crocodiles! Go back to page 13 and let's try that game again.

That's an excellent idea! But what about the tomb you're building for the pharaoh? You know how much your friend loves to tour the pyramid. Maybe if you leave a message, the pharaoh will find it there.

It's getting late in the day, and everyone else has gone home. You have the place to yourself as you sneak to the pyramid and into the burial chamber. A drawing on the wall could be the perfect way to warn the pharaoh!

Draw the pharaoh looking surprised by your warning here. ⟶

I know this is important, so I started the drawing for you!

See this grid? Artists use grids to make sure everything is perfectly proportioned to please the gods. If you draw something correctly, it will come true in the afterlife!

Each grid square is the width of the main figure's hand. Main figures have to be 18 squares high from the bottom of their feet to the hairline. Knees are 6 squares high; shoulders are 16 high and 6 wide.

Draw your figure's head turned to the side with the eye gazing at you. The chest and shoulders look as if they're facing you. The hips are turned to the side. Draw arms, legs, hands, and feet—even the big toes. Your figures should be stiff and shouldn't look relaxed.

Important characters are always drawn full size; everyone else is smaller. Only gods can rival pharaohs in size. Animals can be drawn in any style!

When you're finished, place your finger on the hairline of your drawing. Slide it along the line to the number at the right side of the grid. Turn to that page.

Are you **drawn** to page 125?

Or to page 153?

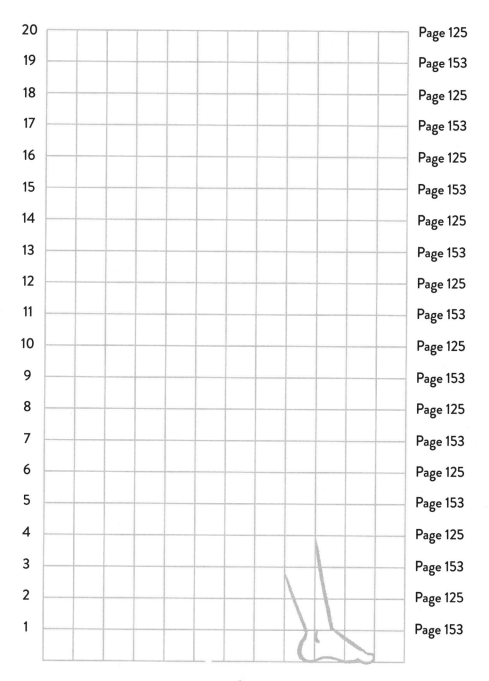

20   Page 125

19   Page 153

18   Page 125

17   Page 153

16   Page 125

15   Page 153

14   Page 125

13   Page 153

12   Page 125

11   Page 153

10   Page 125

9   Page 153

8   Page 125

7   Page 153

6   Page 125

5   Page 153

4   Page 125

3   Page 153

2   Page 125

1   Page 153

Walking to the barge that will take you down the river to work, you think about how you met the pharaoh a few months ago.

The pharaoh likes you! You're both young and you both LOVE animals. Sure, the pharaoh is at the top of the social "pyramid" and you're at the bottom . . . but somehow you've become pals. In fact, your jokes make the pharaoh laugh hard enough to get a stomachache!

But not everyone is excited about your friendship. The vizier, who is kind of like the vice president, does *not* like you. He thinks the pharaoh shouldn't even bother talking to you!

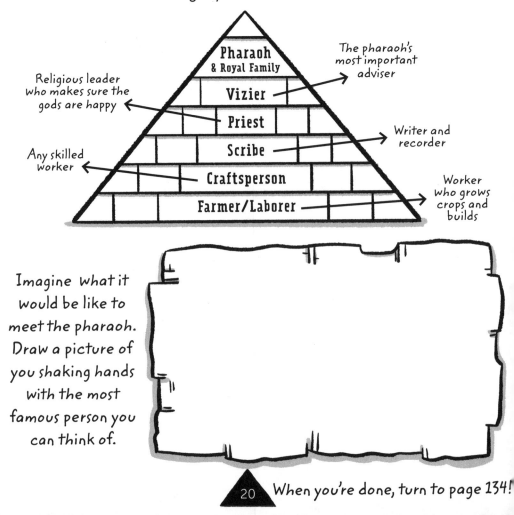

Religious leader who makes sure the gods are happy

The pharaoh's most important adviser

Any skilled worker

Writer and recorder

Worker who grows crops and builds

Pharaoh & Royal Family

Vizier

Priest

Scribe

Craftsperson

Farmer/Laborer

Imagine what it would be like to meet the pharaoh. Draw a picture of you shaking hands with the most famous person you can think of.

When you're done, turn to page 134!

You really don't want to take a nap. But if you don't, the Escape the Underworld game will never start, and you—

Watch out! Something is sneaking up behind you. You feel a sting on your elbow—ouch! What creature do you think just stung you? Draw it here!

If you drew something with wings,
like a bee, turn to page 63.

If you sketched a creature with lots
of legs, like a scorpion, go to page 24.

Something else in the croc's mouth? Go to page 42.

Turn to page 21. Did you draw a boat?

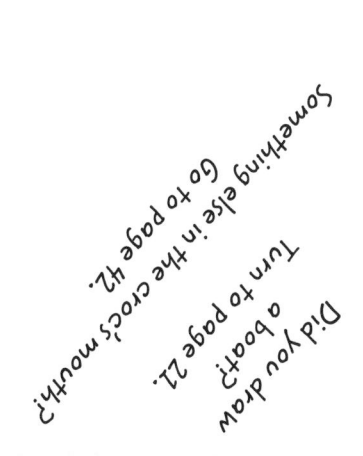

"Go take your royal nap," your mom says. "And when you wake up, you'll be in the game. Good luck, my child!" But you're way too excited to sleep. Maybe playing with a toy on the shelves will calm you down.

What will it be? The paint set, the model boat, the doll with movable arms, the dollhouse with miniature furniture? Or maybe the crocodile pull toy with jaws that open and close?

PAGE 178

One of the toys I just listed is missing! Did Ineni take it? No. Looks like you fed it to the crocodile. Draw the missing toy in its mouth.

When you're done, turn up this flap.

22

Hmm . . . actually, that's not the way it happened!
A spear got close to your dad, but it flew past him. Whew!

A pharaoh needs amazing observation skills—work
on yours here! Circle as many differences
between the two pictures as you can find.

If you're having a tough time, go to page 182 for the answer.

END

After you've circled at least FIVE
differences between the two
pictures, return to page 162 and try
tracking those spears again!

23

Good thing I know part of an ancient Egyptian cure for scorpion stings! Here's all you have to do: Say, "I am the king's child, eldest and first." Now, while the sting is bleeding, immediately lick it with your tongue. Put oil on the bite daily, and soak a strip of linen to place on it, too.

This cure came from the actual Book of the Dead. It's thousands of years old!

Draw a picture of you licking your elbow.

All better? Get back on track. Turn to page 26.

"Move faster!" you order the confused baboon. In a panic, he jumps out of the fig tree, and you see he has something in his paw.

"About time," you say, grabbing the object and taking a bite out of it.

Big mistake. It's actually a rock that the baboon must have grabbed off the ground. It'll be hard to boss people around as a pharaoh—or a kid—without any teeth.

Say goodbye to your dreams of being top ruler!

END

Suddenly, you let out a huge YAWN. Either the sting or the excitement of possibly being pharaoh makes you very tired. You climb into bed and you sleep . . . and sleep. . . .

You hear your mom say "No peeking" as she ties a blindfold over your eyes. But you're really too sleepy to open them anyway.

Arms lift you up, and you are carried out of the room. You know you're safe, and you fall back asleep.

Zzzzzzz . . .

26

Shh. Turn to page 116.

As you take the throne as pharaoh, the sounds that fill your ears are not shouts of *"Your Highness"* or *"You're amazing!"* They are *"Ha! Ha!"* Your people cannot stop laughing. And who can blame them?

After all, you're wearing a chicken on your head!

END

Let's try a more **egg-cellent** outcome! Turn back to page 9.

Bang! The sound of someone dropping a flashlight in the Grand Gallery startles you.

"Eep!" Chione makes a worried sound. "That must be the Venisons. They'll be here any second. We have to find a way out!"

You both rush into the next chamber. It seems to be a dead end. Now you're really trapped!

"Wait," you say. "What's on the walls?"

As you look around the room, you discover medical problems painted over closed doors. In front of each door is a basket. "These baskets should hold ingredients for different cures the pharaoh would need in the afterlife," Chione says. "The door behind one of the baskets must be the way out! But which one?"

You don't have time to try all the doors. Hurry!

Think about the ailment mentioned in the last secret message. What ingredients would you need to cure it? Draw those ingredients in the basket in front of the door.

When you're done, turn to page 118.

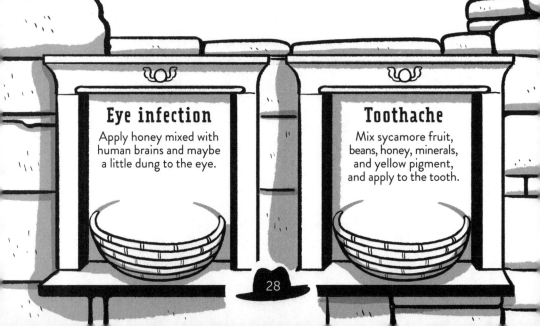

Eye infection

Apply honey mixed with human brains and maybe a little dung to the eye.

Toothache

Mix sycamore fruit, beans, honey, minerals, and yellow pigment, and apply to the tooth.

You gently touch your nose. It doesn't *feel* like your brain was pulled out, does it? And your face and body aren't wrapped in linen. But you do find a scarab beetle amulet on top of your chest.

Without thinking, you toss the amulet from your chest, and it bounces off the wall. "Why am I in a burial chamber?" you wonder out loud. "What is going on?"

Pharaohs believed you really *could* take everything with you. They filled their tombs and pyramids with pets, gold, carts, clothes, boats, games, and jewelry—all things they'd want to enjoy for eternity.

What are two things you would pack for the afterlife? Draw them in the suitcase. Make sure they're your two favorite things. . . . We're talking FOREVER here!

Go to the next page.

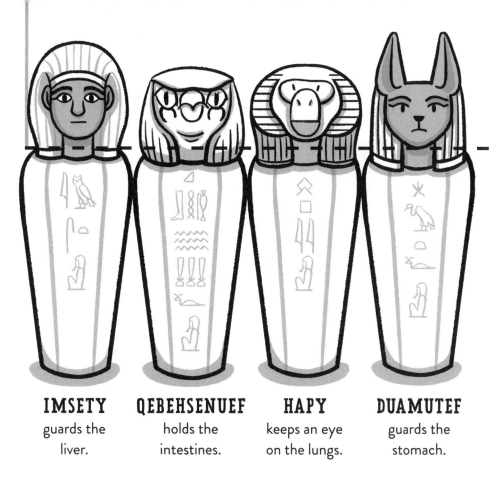

IMSETY
guards the
liver.

QEBEHSENUEF
holds the
intestines.

HAPY
keeps an eye
on the lungs.

DUAMUTEF
guards the
stomach.

Aces! Love those items in your suitcase! However, what people really need to live forever in the afterlife are organs. That's why the lungs, liver, stomach, and intestines are preserved in canopic jars in many Egyptian tombs.

You still have your organs. . . . So what's in the jars at the top of this page? There's only one way to find out. Break open the jars by tearing along the dotted line and folding over the flap.

2   **1**   **4**   **3**

Those aren't organs inside the jars! They're scraps of papyrus. Write each word in the matching numbered blank. What does the message say?

Book of the Dead—turn to page 32.
Dead of the Book—go to page 140.

The Book of the Dead! Yes! That's *exactly* what you need. It will be like a road map to Escape the Underworld!

Okay, this is just a game, but the underworld is NOT a pleasant place. It is filled with lakes of fire, scary caves, and half-human monsters such as Blood-Eater and Demolisher. And Apep, the serpent god of destruction, hides in the shadows and waits to swallow you up!

Oh, and there's a creature called the Devourer. She has the head of a crocodile, the body of a lion, and the back legs of a hippo. Finish the drawing of her here.

32

That *is* pretty terrifying! Run to page 36.

Hmm. Okay, I am up for watching you try this out.

You attempt to walk on your head. Unfortunately, your skull is not skilled in this area! You fall to the ground . . . *SPLAT!* Game over!

END

Let's avoid this headache. Return to page 40 and try again!

Um, there is no easy way to say this. . . . Close your eyes if you want!

Your heart is weighed down by wrongdoing! Anubis throws it to the floor. Tear along the dotted line and fold over the flap to see who is waiting to devour it.

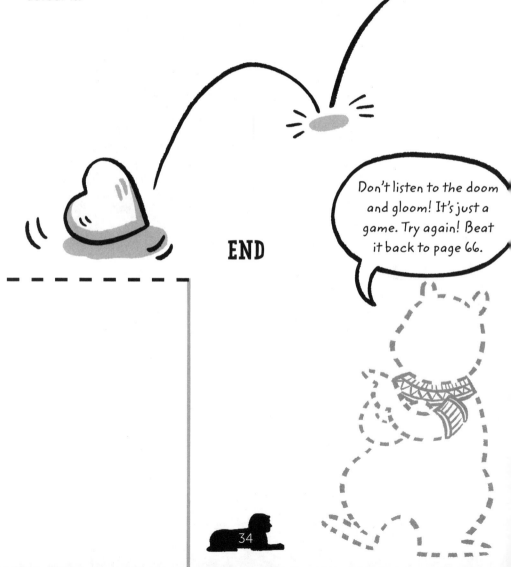

END

Don't listen to the doom and gloom! It's just a game. Try again! Beat it back to page 66.

"Aaaah!" you shout as you stumble into a giant monster crocodile. You turn to run, but you don't even know where you are!

"My child!" your mom says, shaking you out of your daze.

Talk about LOST in thought! You got confused just *thinking* about the maze of the underworld.

END

Don't worry! Let's be **a-maze-ing** and give that another shot. Turn back to page 133!

Aces, my brave friend!

Luckily, your dad ordered the scribe to make a Book of the Dead especially for you.

Actually, the *book* is a *scroll*—rolled-up paper made of papyrus. And the paper is filled with magic spells, hints, directions, and passwords you'll need to get past creepy challenges in this game. It's as if you've been given all the answers to the quizzes and tests in school . . . before you take them!

This Book of the Dead belongs to

_____ .

Write in your name here.

As you unroll the Book of the Dead, you see that it isn't finished! You read from left to right, or right to left. It might depend on which way the animal heads are facing.

On this scroll is spell #76, which will help you fight off snakes. It lets you turn into any creature you want to be so that you can get through the underworld challenge!

Draw yourself here

and here.

When you're done, turn to page 41.

CHOMP!

Apep the hungry snake closes his huge jaws around you—and everything goes black! Um, it will be hard to be pharaoh for a day when you're inside a serpent's mouth. Just saying . . .

As you wait for your dad to come and get you out, you have time to think about your last decision.

END

Hoof it over to page 43!

Let's redraw the past on page 45! Just remember you're one cool cat!

Head over to page 33!

Fold over the flap that names the body part in the spell on page 41....
Actually, before you follow the directions, draw yourself eating a spaghetti dinner and drinking fruit punch while upside down.

Wrote feet?
Flip this flap.

If you wrote the word head, turn this flap.

Hold. On. What is happening? Why are you standing on your head? Oh! I know!

Many Egyptians worried they would travel through the underworld upside down. I guess that's happened to you! This might be a good time for you to use your Book of the Dead! Try using spell #51. It's the formula for putting everything right side up.

But first you need to fix the spell. It's backward. Use a mirror (or just your brain) and rewrite the spell in the right direction here!

ℲEEⱯ ЯUOY NO ꓘⱢAW UOY YAM
MAY YOU NOT WALK UPSIDE DOWN

If you get stuck, go to page 182 for the answer.

Go to page 40.

41

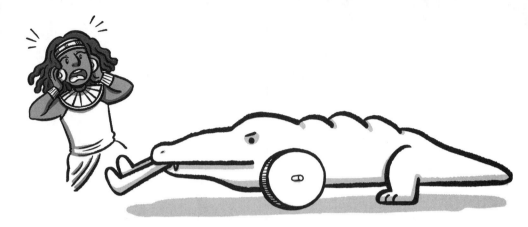

Just then, Ineni walks into your room and sees the doll's legs sticking out of the crocodile's mouth. "Oh no!" she yells, and runs out of the room before you can explain that you made a mistake. Ineni will probably tell everyone you plan to feed people to the crocodiles in the Nile River when you're pharaoh!

I'm sad to say, you'll never be ruler for a day now!

END

Let's find an ending that floats your boat! Turn back to page 22 and try again.

I have good news and bad news.
Before I tell you anything, draw
something that makes you happy
in the bubble over your head.
You're going to need it!

The good news is that you're right side up. (Thank you! That was making me extremely dizzy!)

And now for the bad news. Remember when I mentioned Apep, the giant snake and god of destruction? The one that's super long and has a head made of hard rock? The one called the Evil Lizard, He Who Spits, the Destroyer, and the Eater-Up of Souls?

43

Um, how do
I say this?
I guess I'll
just show
you. Fold
over this
flap.

Apep's right behind you! Turn to page 45.

So . . . it's tough for me to tell you this, but flying machines won't be invented for a few thousand years. Needless to say, you don't get far before technology catches up with you and brings you crashing back down to earth!

END

Maybe your last idea didn't fly. But your next one will soar! Zoom back to page 15 and try taking off again!

Are you ready to battle the evil, miles-long snake?

Don't forget that spell #76 in your Book of the Dead lets you turn into any creature you want to be! What will you choose to be? Draw it here!

I've got a tidbit in my Escapologist Files that might help you!

PAGE
176

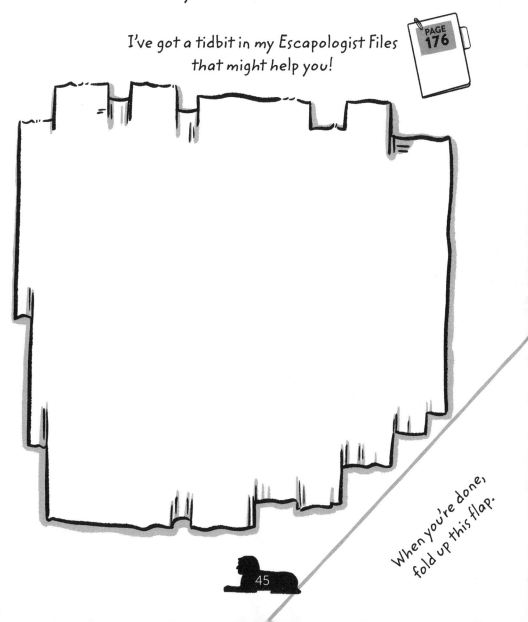

When you're done, fold up this flap.

45

You did it! Your catlike shape scared off Apep...
for now, anyway. He slithered into the shadows of the
underworld. But I can guarantee that he will be back.

You've arrived at the Hall of Justice! Ma'at, the goddess of truth and justice, is in charge of this impressive place, but many gods hang around here. Spell #125 in the Book of the Dead tells you what to say when you meet the god Osiris at the door. Say these words out loud: "Behold, I have come to you, I have brought you truth, I have repelled falsehood for you."

I must admit, you sound like an amazing superhero!
Draw yourself as a defender of justice.

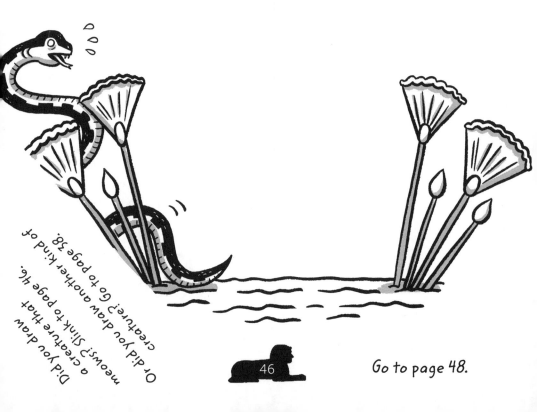

Did you draw a creature that meows? Slink to page 46. Or did you draw another kind of creature? Go to page 58.

Go to page 48.

You've arrived at your destination! Time to go ashore!

"Help me get that stone onto the dock," you order the oarsmen.

You should probably leave the bossing around to me. As the stone is being unloaded, someone rocks the barge. (Okay, okay, it was me!) You accidentally tumble into the Nile!

You bathe often in the river, and your clothes are washed in the Nile, too. But you didn't want to do both of those things at the same time!

Draw yourself inside a giant washing machine.

*Wasn't that **loads** of fun? Go to page 141.*

The god Osiris is impressed, too. He moves aside to let you into the Hall of Justice. But the second you step inside . . . the floor shoots up at an angle and you are knocked back.

"I will not let you tread on me!" shouts the floor of the Hall of Justice in a deep voice.

Once you get over the fact that the floor is *talking*, you need to figure out what to say to it. You check the Book of the Dead.

"Why not?" you ask the floor, just as the book instructs. "I am pure."

"Because I do not know the names of your feet, with which you would tread on me," the floor says. "Tell them to me."

You have to name your feet to cross the floor.

I think you should get in the right frame of mind for this **feat**. What if the world were populated by feet instead of people? Please draw them in this scene for me. (I've done one for you in the boat on the Nile!)

When you're finished, tiptoe to page 51.

Does the front of your boat look like this?

If no, turn to page 96.

If yes, go to page 126.

You make it to the banks of the Nile, right where your mom discovered the other parts of the solar boat.

Archaeologists spent about ten years putting together the boat from the Great Pyramid. YOU HAVE TWO MINUTES to assemble this one before Dr. Venison and James catch up!

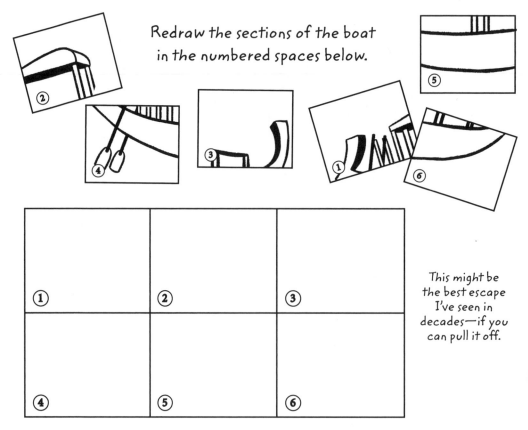

Redraw the sections of the boat in the numbered spaces below.

This might be the best escape I've seen in decades—if you can pull it off.

When you've finished this boat,
tear along the dotted lines, and fold this flap up.

50

Aces! Ready to name your feet now? First, read this joke out loud.

Q: What did the sneaker salesperson tell the actors?

A: The **shoe** must go on!

Draw your face here after reading that joke, and fill in the speech bubble, writing either the word "Ha" or the word "Ugh."

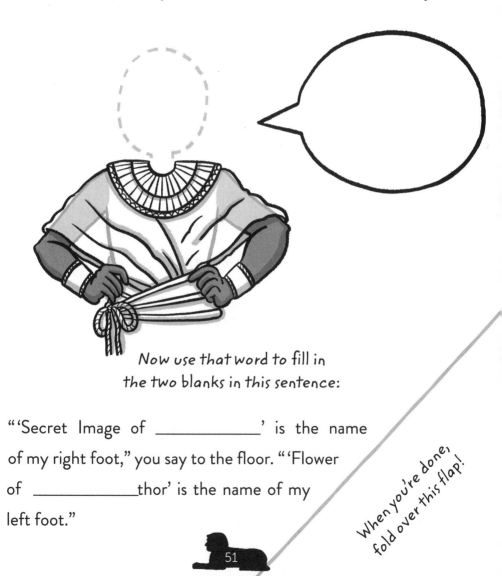

Now use that word to fill in the two blanks in this sentence:

" 'Secret Image of _____' is the name of my right foot," you say to the floor. " 'Flower of _____thor' is the name of my left foot."

So you didn't like my joke? I would like to see you try and do better! Without looking ahead, write the name of a fruit here _____ and your favorite kind of ice cream

Word #1

here _____. Use them in the joke I wrote below!

Word #2

You: Knock, knock.

Me: Who's there?

You: _____ _____.

Word #1   Word #2

Me: _____ _____ who?

Word #1   Word #2

You: _____ _____. Isn't the

Word #1   Word #2

Master Escapologist amazing?

END

Now I'm saying "Ugh"! Laugh your way back to page 51 and try "Ha" this time.

Did you write the word Ha? Go to page 114.

Did you write Ugh? Turn to page 52.

"What else do the hieroglyphs say to do?" you ask your sister.

Chione rereads the writing. "We need to open the lids of two of the coffins in just the right way, and then another message will be revealed."

For extra protection, mummies were often placed inside one coffin, and that coffin was put inside a second coffin, and then another.

"Be careful," your sister warns as you reach toward the outer coffin. "If you trigger a trap, the whole ceiling could cave in."

You move very carefully. And you do it! You reach the final coffin without the ceiling collapsing! Before you open it, you take a second to wonder about the mummy you'll discover inside. Pharaohs were really into their image. They wanted to be remembered in history as being fit and toned.

PAGE 178

Um, guess what you find inside? NOTHING! It's empty!

"Wait a second," Chione says. "Maybe it's not totally empty. Is that another hint from the pyramid worker?"

It IS another message. What does it say?

THE 👩‍⚕️ + 'S 🧒 F + 6 - S

IS A 🚪 TO THE TRUE ✴️

Not sure what it says? Turn to page 182.

Did you read the word MOTHER?
Turn to page 103.

53

Did you see the word BREAK?
Go to page 101.

HALL OF

NEB-MAAT

SET-QESU

ARI-EM-AB-F

UTU-NESERT

55

WELCOME HALL OF

In this hall, you will be judged by 42 gods. To get out of here in one piece, you'll have to call each god by his or her name and tell each one that you did NOT do a certain bad thing. And you have to do it ALL from memory!

You have to remember 42 gods and sins? I'm probably the most intelligent genius on the planet, and even I would have a tough time with that!

It's a good thing the scribe added a cheat sheet to your Book of the Dead. It lists the gods in the correct order. But the scribe only got to 33. . . . Uh-oh.

TO THE TRUTH!

You're going to have to get to know these on your own. Here's what you do:

1. Fold and tear these two pages so that they look like this:

2. Use the flaps like underworld flash cards!

3. Can you memorize the things you have to tell each god you did NOT do?

After you can recognize the gods' names, turn to page 60.

I have not told lies.

TEAR HERE

I have not stolen land.

TEAR HERE

I have not been angry without cause.

TEAR HERE

I have not disobeyed the law.

FOLD HERE

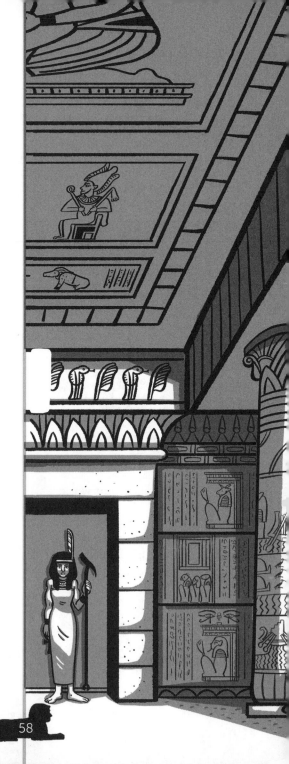

NEBA

UNEM-BESEK

SERTIU

KHEMIU

TRUTH

Excellent! You have only one more god to go!

Um, I hate to mention it, but the confession for this god is "I did not make anyone cry." Does the name Ineni ring a bell? Didn't you just make her cry by laughing at her?

If this last god thinks you're lying, he'll kick you out of the Hall of Truth and back into the waiting jaws of Apep.

Maybe you should draw a bouquet of flowers for Ineni as an apology.

Go to the next page.

That's very kind. But actually you didn't need to do that. Remember that scarab beetle amulet you woke up with? It can get you out of this.

You can either go all the way back to the burial chamber on page 30 and get it . . . or just draw it here. The Egyptians of your time believe that when you draw something, it becomes real in the afterlife—as long as you do it *right*.

Draw the scarab beetle.

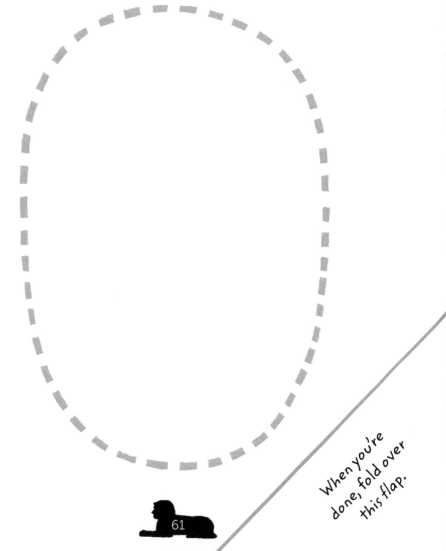

When you're done, fold over this flap.

61

Remember how I mentioned that whatever you draw on the walls in the burial chamber will come true? Well, guess what. You just created a new kind of beetle.

And it happens to be six stories tall.

You might want to use those legs of yours ... and run!

END

Don't let this ending **bug** you! Go back to page 61 and give your beetle at least six legs!

Does your bug have 0 to 5 legs? Scuttle to page 62. Or 6 or more legs? Beat it to page 64.

Without looking, you turn and swat at the flying insect that stung you.
SMACK! You miss the bug. But you connect with the face of the vizier!

He's your dad's right-hand man. He's VERY powerful, and right now he is extremely unhappy. You can just tell by the look in his eyes that he will NEVER allow you to become pharaoh—not for a day or even for a second!

END

That really stings! Fly back to page 21 and draw a scorpion instead.

Well done! That's close enough.
Tear the dotted line to flip over
the amulet and read the spell
on its underside.

You might want to hurry.
I think the god is getting impatient.

That's a handy spell! It will hide from the gods all your mistakes and the bad stuff you might have done, by making those deeds invisible. At least I hope so!

Fingers crossed. Turn to page 66.

Hmm. That's not quite right, is it? This should be the END. But I will cut you some slack . . . just this once.

To figure out what to do next, draw what you see in the boxes in the correct parts of the grid. When you're done, follow the instructions.

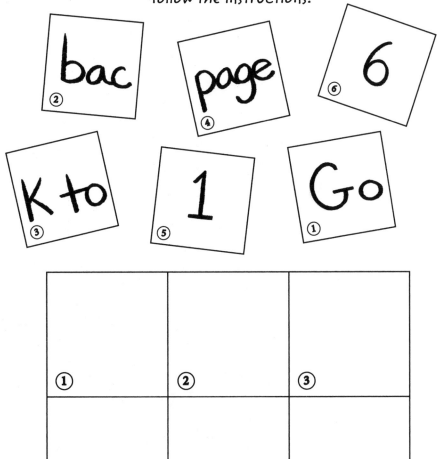

Stuck? Don't panic! Go to page 182 for help.

The spell worked! The gods nod and say together, "You may pass."

You're allowed into the Hall of Judgment. This is the last and biggest test of all.

Here the god Anubis will weigh your heart against a white feather of Truth on a scale.

What weighs more? Your heart? Or the feather? Draw a heart on one side of the scale and a feather on the other. You choose!

VERY IMPORTANT: Check out my Escapologist Files in the back of this book before making your decision! Remember that Devourer you drew? She's waiting to eat your heart if you make the wrong choice—and then you'll NEVER win the game.

PAGE
177

If your heart is heavier, fold over this flap.

If your heart is lighter, flip this flap.

67

Go to page 34.

Excellent! You've escaped Apep! Ra takes you to the god Osiris, who allows you into the afterlife: the Field of Reeds. This is para- dise! It looks a lot like the Nile near your family's palace. You glance around. The whole point of paradise is that you're reunited with family.

But you don't see anyone. You do see a row of shabti dolls. These figures will come to life and work in the fields, prepare food, and do other chores so that you can relax and enjoy paradise. Normally they are doll-size miniatures. But these figures are life-size.

Your heart is free of wrongdoing! Continue toward paradise! Turn to page 15.

Go to the next page.

Start tearing here! ↗

Say spell #6—the formula for making the figures do work in the afterlife—from the Book of the Dead as you tear along the dotted line and fold the strip like the example below. When the shabti doll springs to life, look at the back of the doll for where to go next.

SPELL #6
OH, SHABTI!

Do all

the work

that needs

to be done!

Stop tearing here! ↗

Turn to page 70.

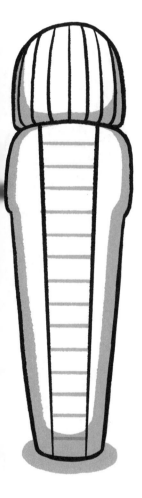

After you say the spell, you hear laughter from one of the dolls—laughter that sounds very familiar. The doll reaches up and removes a mask from its face.

It's your father! He's smiling as he gives you a giant hug. This really is paradise!

Soon all the other dolls are removing their masks. Wait a second . . . is that your mother? And the scribe! And Ineni and your nanny! And there are the members of the pyramid work crew that you love. . . . Well, almost all of them. One is missing, but you'll ask about that worker later. Right now you're too excited to even think straight.

"I'm sorry if the game got a little scary," your father says. "We wanted to make sure you learned the importance of being kind and good, not only as a human being but as a ruler, too!"

"Did you learn your lesson?" your mom asks you.

"I hope so," you say. "But I have to check with my best friend first. Don't I, Ineni?"

70

Go to the next page.

Ineni shrugs. "Who's your best friend?"

"It's you," you say, and give her a hug. "Can you forgive me for laughing at you?"

Ineni seems too surprised to speak for a second. Then she grins and answers, "Don't worry about it."

"Thanks," you say, and turn back to your parents. "But what about this tomb you used to trick me? Who is it for?"

"Oh, we'll probably just leave it empty," your father says. "It will keep the grave robbers scratching their heads!"

"Aren't you going to ask about your prize for winning the game? Or have you really changed that much?" Ineni teases.

"No way!" you respond. "When does my day as the pharaoh begin?"

Right now. Turn to page 108.

marble

Well done! You're skilled at making a mummy!

Chione loves mummies. To give her a break from worrying about escape, you ask, "Why were mummies wrapped so tight?"

"Because they didn't know how to relax and unwind!" she jokes. Then she gets more serious. "If a person wanted to have a good afterlife, their body had to go into the underworld undisturbed by grave robbers."

You nod. "That's why the punishment for tomb raiding was death! Builders often put in fake doors, secret passages, and traps to protect the dead. But they rarely worked—"

"I think I know a trap that worked," your sister interrupts. She's looking over your shoulder with wide eyes.

Matches

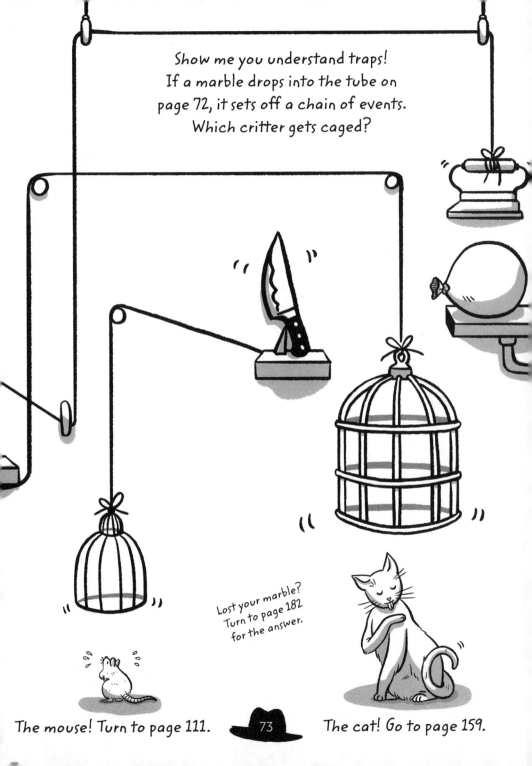

Show me you understand traps!
If a marble drops into the tube on
page 72, it sets off a chain of events.
Which critter gets caged?

Lost your marble?
Turn to page 182
for the answer.

The mouse! Turn to page 111.

The cat! Go to page 159.

ACES! You've made your escape!

Track your progress as you finish escaping each possible path.

Draw the pyramid worker here.

Draw the pharaoh for a day here.

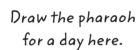

Draw the archaeologist kid here.

I have a secret to share . . . but only with someone who has the potential to be a great escapologist. Prove **you're** that someone! Turn back to page 7 to try another path. When you've completed ALL THREE paths—and only then!—turn to page 184.

ARCHAEOLOGIST PATH

Welcome, tomb explorer, to the night of your life!

I cannot guarantee that you will escape the night . . . but good luck! This is the only path that takes place in the present day.

Before we go any further, I need you to take a Tomb Test.

Imagine you've triggered a booby trap inside an ancient tomb. The boulder rolling your way is moving faster than a speeding car. What do you do? Choose either A or B—quick!—and fold over that flap.

A.
Find a way to
escape . . . and RUN!
Fold this flap.

B.
Find a way to stop the
boulder . . . and STAND
YOUR GROUND!
Fold this flap.

77

Aces! You might just have what it takes to escape this adventure after all.*
Go to the next page.

Draw a ladder to get out! Turn the page when you get up here.

Draw a wall to block the boulder! When you're done, turn the page.

*Actually, either A or B would have worked. But you made a rock-solid choice!

Your mom is an archaeologist. She's here in the Valley of the Kings to uncover more about a young pharaoh whose tomb—and mummy!—have never been found.

PAGE 176

You and the missing pharaoh have the same name. This ruler was also known as the Pharaoh of Beasts, thanks to a love of animals.

Your mom has found four of the five pieces of a solar boat about a mile away, near the Nile River. Ancient Egyptians believed the pharaoh could use the boat in the afterlife to sail across the sky with the god Ra. Your mom knows that her discovery of the pieces means a tomb must be nearby.

PAGE 177

Start at Site A and connect the pyramids that your mom has explored. What number is revealed? Write it in the blank below.

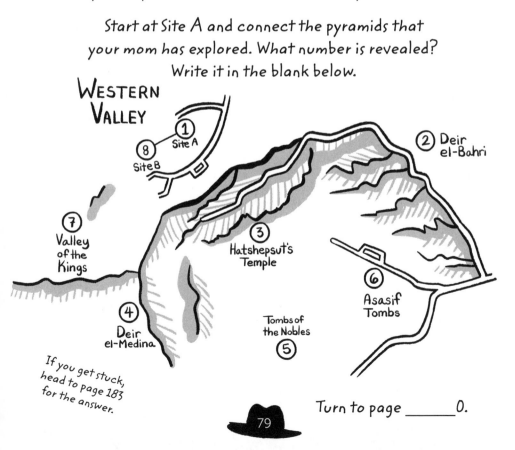

WESTERN VALLEY

① Site A
⑧ Site B
② Deir el-Bahri
⑦ Valley of the Kings
③ Hatshepsut's Temple
⑥ Asasif Tombs
④ Deir el-Medina
Tombs of the Nobles ⑤

If you get stuck, head to page 183 for the answer.

Turn to page _____ 0.

Not everyone agrees that your mom will find the missing boat piece or the ancient tomb. Dr. Venison and his son James are in charge of the dig. At the campsite, you overhear them telling your mom she is way off track. They plan to shut down the expedition! Your mom is trying to change their minds.

Maybe you can help your mom by finding an artifact.

Even though it's nighttime, you decide to walk to the dig site along the Nile. The darkness provides great cover for hidden danger, like a hungry crocodile or a cranky hippopotamus. In fact, you think you hear something in the grass just behind you. . . .

Draw what it might be.

Did you draw a vampire penguin?
No—turn to page 138. Yes—go to page 165.

Good choice! Dr. Venison and James went the wrong way . . . *down*. They must be thinking about where many other cultures bury the dead: deep in the ground. Meanwhile, you and your sister are heading *up* to the burial chamber.

Chione has a spring in her step, and you know why. Yes, you're running from bad guys, but you're lucky, too! You're exploring a tomb that has been undisturbed for thousands of years! Suddenly, the narrow passage opens up. The ceiling soars overhead.

Oh! You're in the Grand Gallery! Draw yourself climbing to the top of the passage. When you're done, turn to page 97.

Those servants don't have a choice about the work they're doing. I'm very sorry to say that there are enslaved people in ancient Egypt. Turn to the back to read more.

PAGE 180

Like you, many of the construction workers who are building the pyramids are not enslaved. You have a better life than a lot of people. You get a place to sleep. You receive food as payment: wheat, barley, fresh fish, fruit, vegetables, and a gallon or so of beer, which everyone drinks—even kids.

And sometimes you get delicious, fresh-baked bread seasoned with honey . . . and some sand. There's no escaping the sand from the surrounding desert. It gets into everything and wears down the teeth of all Egyptians!

Draw the teeth in this mouth after it's been eating sand sandwiches for ten years. Then turn to page 47.

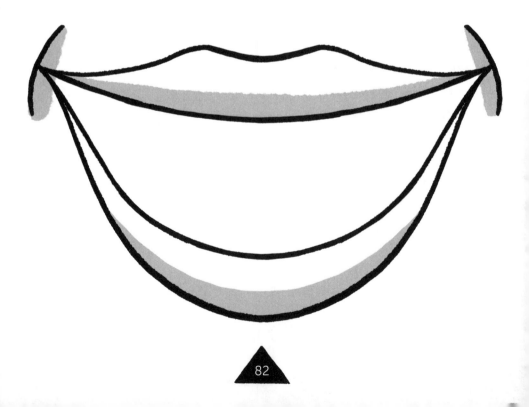

Yes, there is evidence that people have been making popcorn for thousands of years, BUT this tomb is not filled with it.

END

All right, your decision made me laugh, so I am going to give you a free pass on that one.

Before you return to page 86 and try again, work up an appetite by finding all 11 pieces of popcorn hidden in this picture.

Need help? Turn to page 183 for the answer.

Well done! Clearly, brains run in your family.

"Don't even bother telling me to go back to camp," Chione says. "I'm staying. And if we're going to find the missing piece of the boat, we'll need these." She holds out the bag of tools your mom taught you to use at a dig site.

"Okay," you say. "Let's get to work."

You start digging with the small hand shovel. When you feel it tap something in the ground, you stop immediately. You use a brush to swipe away the dirt. Now the really delicate work begins! To avoid damaging an ancient object, you switch to the "dentist tools," like tiny picks and toothbrushes. You can never be too careful when it comes to digging up the past!

Go to the next page to prove that you have
a gentle touch and can dig by "feel" with the tools.
Follow my directions and be careful! If you dig
too fast, you may damage an artifact.

Dig Directions

1. Turn to page 87 and put the tip of your pen on the START HERE dot. Keep your writing hand in place there.

2. With your *other* hand, use this page to cover your writing hand so that you can't see what you'll draw on page 87. Look at the ruler on this page to help you estimate length. And don't lift your pen from the paper till you've finished all the steps!

3. Draw a two-inch line going straight up.

4. Draw an inch-long line to the right.

5. Draw a line that goes up half an inch.

6. Draw a half-inch-long line to the right.

7. Draw a straight line down half an inch.

8. From there, draw a diagonal line down and to the left to connect to the dot where you started.

When you're done drawing, turn to page 87 to see what you've found in the ground!

Finally you reach the bottom of the hill. You tumble into the pitch dark. Shining the flashlight on your phone toward your sister, you ask, "Are you okay, Chione?"

"Yes," she says. "But you're the worst sled ever!"

When you try to call for help, you discover that the phone has no service this far underground. You shine your flashlight around the space. You're in some kind of huge cave.

What do you see in the beam of light?
I'll give you a hint: It's either lots and lots of cats . . .
or thousands of pounds of popcorn.
Draw what you see here!

If you see cats, turn to page 93.

If you spot popcorn, flip to page 83.

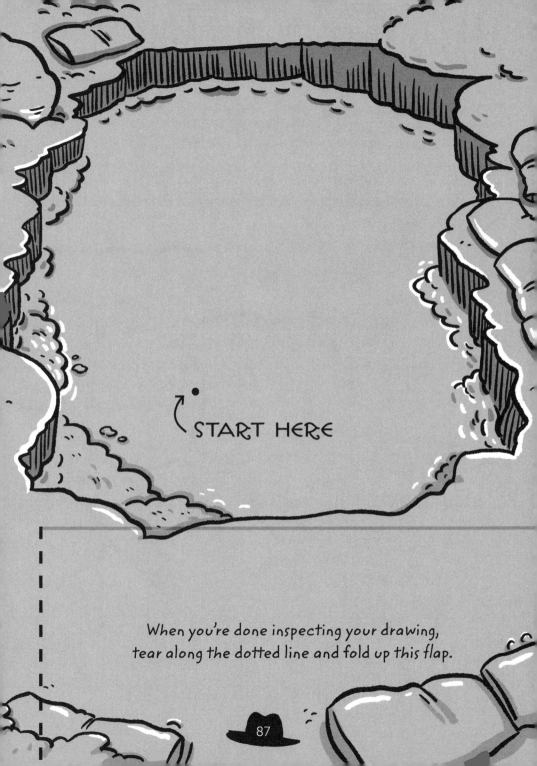

START HERE

When you're done inspecting your drawing,
tear along the dotted line and fold up this flap.

Oh my. I'm not sure what that thing is.

To see whether you've found the last part of the solar boat, you take the object, jump into the Nile River, and . . .

You instantly sink to the bottom!

END

You're not sunk yet! I'll give you the right piece so you can sail ahead to page 89.

Turn to page 89.

Turn the page!

or this?

. . . this . . .

Does what you drew look more like . . .

I can't believe it!
You just made a major discovery!

"It's the missing piece of the solar boat!" your sister shouts. "We found it!"

"Shh," you tell her. You're not sure why, but you have the feeling you're being watched.

"We should take it to Mom right away," Chione whispers.

"Not yet," you respond. "First we have to take a picture. Where an object is found is very important!"

You want the picture of the artifact to be as perfect as possible, so you remove the foldable tripod from the bag of tools. The tripod will keep the camera steady. Uh-oh. One of the legs pokes through the ground.

What is that down there? Use your pen to poke through until you can see a number. Then flip to that page.

Poke here

You and your sister zoom downward.

"Watch out for that hole!" Chione shouts.

But it's too late. You can't change direction that fast. In a flash, both of you fall into the hole with a *thud.* It's dark and creepy here.

"Now what?" Chione asks nervously.

Um, any ideas, Amicus?

END

That's too scary for me! Return to page 92 and give it another shot.

With your sister crouched next to you, you shine your phone's flashlight down into the hole. It looks like there is a layer of strong plaster just under the surface of dirt. It's dark down there, and you gently push open the hole a bit more.

Color in the circle so you can't see the numbers.

"All that digging is not a good idea!" Chione says.

You should listen to your sister.

Suddenly, the ground around the hole collapses and you fall into the earth. Chione is right behind you!

Turn the page!

You spin and land flat on your stomach, facing down a steep hill. Your sister falls onto your back. *Umph!*

"Sorry!" she shouts.

With your sister on top of you, you whiz downhill like an out-of-control sled.

It's too dark! I can't see what's happening. Draw the path you two take through the maze.

When you reach the bottom, turn to the page number at the end of the path.

START

Page 86

92

Page 90

"Whoa!" Chione says. "There must be a few thousand cat mummies here!"

"A *few* thousand?" you ask, stunned.

"Oh, that's nothing!" your sister says. "One tomb was found with *eighty* thousand cats buried inside. They were meant to keep the pharaoh company in the afterlife."

Cats were treated like gods. When they died, many were mummified like pharaohs so they could enjoy the afterlife, too.

You see that one cat's mummy wrapping has come undone. You know that the bandages of a human mummy can be as long as half a mile.

Imagine the pen or pencil in your hand is a cat. Tear along the strip of paper at the side of the page and then wrap it around the pen or pencil like this.

Use the letters and numbers you reveal to fill in the blanks.

TURN TO _ _ _ _ _ _ _ _.

If you get stuck, head to page 183.

PAGE 180

Yum! The fig is delicious!

"Your Highness!" a young woman calls to you as she rushes into the royal garden. It's Sitre, the nanny who has cared for you since you were a baby. Now Sitre looks very worried. Without another word, she leads you through the palace to the chambers of your mother, Queen Ahmose.

Lying on the couch where she greets official visitors, your mom takes your hand. She says your name and then explains, "I have something to tell you about your father, the great king Tuthmosis." Before you continue, fill in the blanks to find out what your mother calls you.

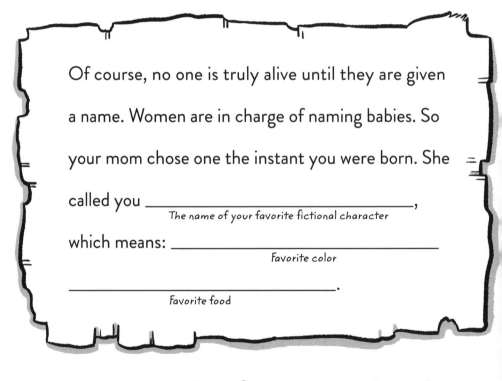

Of course, no one is truly alive until they are given a name. Women are in charge of naming babies. So your mom chose one the instant you were born. She called you _____,
The name of your favorite fictional character

which means: _____
Favorite color

_____.
Favorite food

What is your mom's news? The suspense is killing me!
Turn to page 16, turn to page 16!

It's an army of marching cat mummies!

"Hold on," Chione says. "The pharaoh Mom's searching for was known as the Pharaoh of Beasts, right? We might be close to his tomb!"

Just as you start to respond—

Bright lights click on above. After being in the dark, you feel like someone has turned on the sun. You squint as you look up.

Connect the dots. One picture uses numbers; the other, letters. When things come into focus, decide which flap to fold over.

Not sure what you see? Turn to page 183.

It's two people!

Um. That would be no. Try again!

"Hurry, Chione, get on the boat!" you tell your sister. When she hesitates, you yell, "Jump in!"

She finally hops aboard. You push the boat out on the water and then climb on board, too. Off you go!

For about two feet.

Unfortunately, you put the boat together wrong. And it sinks almost instantly!

END

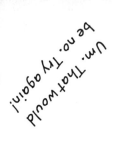

Let's go for smoother sailing! Return to page 50.

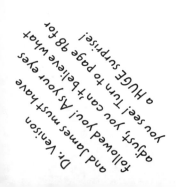

Dr. Venison and James must have followed you! As your eyes adjust you see! Turn to page 98 for a HUGE surprise! you can't believe what

Aces! You've made it to the center of the pyramid . . . the burial chamber!

The picture on the wall in front of you shows how the person buried here wanted to spend eternity—with lots of music and dancing! Some pharaohs chose drawings of servants, or games, or delicious food.

What would you put on your walls? Draw it here.

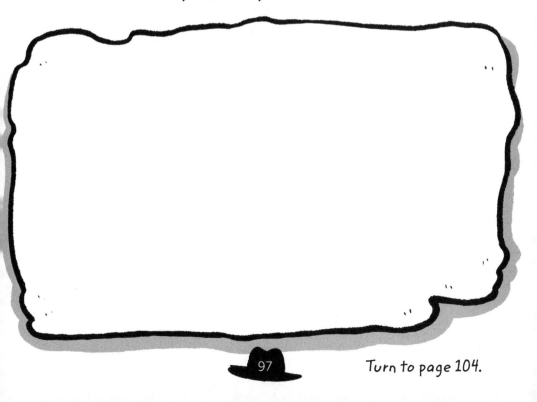

97

Turn to page 104.

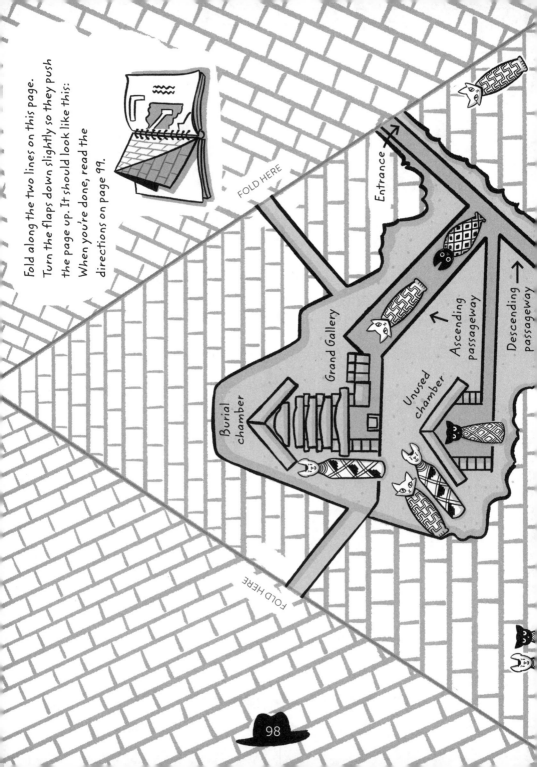

Fold along the two lines on this page. Turn the flaps down slightly so they push the page up. It should look like this: When you're done, read the directions on page 99.

FOLD HERE

Entrance

Descending passageway

Ascending passageway

Unused chamber

Grand Gallery

Burial chamber

FOLD HERE

98

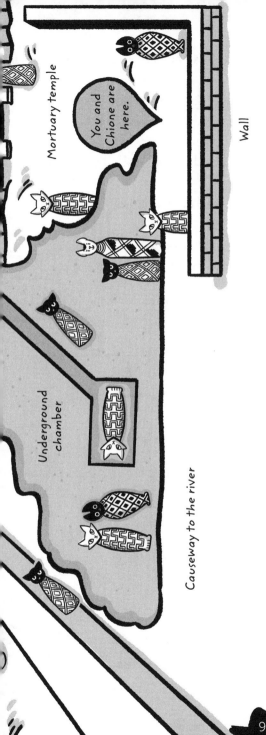

Mortuary temple

You and Chione are here.

Wall

Underground chamber

Causeway to the river

Your Directions

1. Search for the cat mummies that look exactly like this → on these two pages.

2. How many did you find? Write that number here and finish the problem.

103 - _____ = _____

← This is the page you should turn to next!

Stuck?
Peek at page 183.

99

Somehow this massive pyramid complex has remained hidden underground for centuries!

Suddenly you hear whizzing sounds above. You look up and see James and his dad rappelling on ropes through the hole. They're wearing helmets with lights and dropping down directly over you and Chione.

"I told you that archaeologist was onto something, James!" Dr. Venison says as he zips toward the ground.

"Yes!" James calls back to his dad. "We'll steal everything we can lay our hands on, and she'll never know it!"

Those two are tomb raiders! You and your sister have to hide! But where? You can't climb up the outside of the pyramid. They'll spot you.

I don't see a door in the pyramid.
But you can draw one here.

Finished? Turn to page 102.

"The message says to *break* something," you say. "Well, here goes!"

You raise your hand to smash it down on the coffin.

"No!" Chione shouts. "Wait!"

Too late. Your hand is already coming down. As it connects with the coffin, it triggers a booby trap, and stones above you fall. One narrowly misses your head, but it traps your arm inside the coffin—just like the tomb raider next to you was trapped.

Well, at least you'll have company over the centuries!

Time to break that bad ending. Return to page 53.

Well done! You duck inside the pyramid,
out of sight . . . for the moment!

"Now what?" your sister asks you. "We're stuck in here! They'll find us for sure."

"Not if I can help it," you answer. You move the beam of your light around until you find something interesting on the wall.

Builders of the pyramids were proud of their work. The crew often left "signatures"—and sometimes even messages. What does this one say?

I translated the ancient Egyptian into a rebus. Now you turn it into English. (What? You don't expect me to do everything, do you?)

FIND THE 🔑 2 YOUR

ES + IN − L

THE + IN.

Not sure what it says? Turn to page 183.

Did you see the word MUMMY?

If yes, turn to page 139.

102

No? Go to page 132.

The message reads: *The doctor's stomachache fix is a door to the true mother star.*

"Hmm," you say. "'The doctor's stomachache fix?' What does that mean? Did they even have doctors back then?"

"The first known doctor in history was an ancient Egyptian named Hesy-Ra," Chione says. "Hesy-Ra wrote prescriptions and treated illnesses, just like modern doctors do."

She's right. Doctors thought evil spirits and demons could make people sick. So they would say spells, but they also knew how to set broken bones, mix herbs into medicines to fight infections, and perform minor surgeries with sharpened rocks.

PAGE
178

Think of the last time you were sick. Now draw a lucky charm that you could wear on a necklace to prevent the illness from coming back.

When you're done, turn to page 28.

That looks simply amazing!
Maybe I'll stop by your afterlife for the party!

"Look!" Your sister points to another wall in the chamber. The drawings show how mummies are made. Want to give it a try?

Go to the next page.

How to Make a Mummy

As you read each step, tear or carefully use scissors to cut along the dotted lines all the way to the center of the book. Then fold the strip back.

- -

1. Use water from the Nile River and wine to clean the body.

- -

2. Remove all the organs. Stick a hook up the nose, wiggle it around, and pull out the brain. Throw it away.

- -

3. Clean the liver, intestines, stomach, and lungs, and put them into special containers called canopic jars. The lids look like the gods who watch over the organs.

- -

4. Because the heart is the home of intelligence, put it back into the body. To dry out and preserve the body, fill the inside with a special salt called natron—and use it to cover up the body. Leave it alone for about 40 days to dry out.

- -

5. Dig out all the natron and replace it with rags, spices, and plants so that the body keeps its shape. Wrap the body in strips of fancy linen. Be sure to include lucky charms with the wrapping, and say spells that will make them powerful in the afterlife.

- -

6. Place the wrapped body into a coffin. Put that coffin inside another coffin. And so on. When you're all done, put everything in a tomb and seal it tight to protect it from grave robbers!

You did it!
Turn to page 72!

You grab the part of the ancient boat and . . . you and your sister RUN!

But can you outrace the bad guys to the water?

Flip a coin. If you get heads, move ahead one space; tails, move ahead two. Take turns with the bad guys—they automatically move ahead one space on each turn! Make a little X to mark where you and the bad guys land. Don't let them get in front of you or catch up!

Keep trying until you make it to the Nile River first.
Then turn to page 50!

Welcome to

You're the leader of the most important empire in the world! Draw yourself in all the amazing places around Egypt.

Your Day as Pharaoh!

When you're done,
turn to page 74.

You hop onto the litter, take a seat, and shout, "Go, go, go!"

You wait for the wind to rush through your hair as you race down the street, away from the vizier and his guards.

And you wait. And wait. But you haven't moved an inch.

Did you forget that I said you need four people
to carry you on the litter? You're the closest thing to
a sitting duck I have ever seen.

The guards grab you and haul you off.

END

Don't get carried away! Return to page 125 and try again!

You turn to see what Chione is talking about. On the other side of the room, there's a skeleton! One arm is reaching toward the coffin, but the rest of the body is buried under a huge rock slab.

PAGE 179

"That grave robber must have triggered a booby trap," your sister says. "The ceiling caved in, and the thief got stuck underneath."

"Unfortunately," you say, "we need to get into that coffin. The message said that's where we'll find the key to our escape."

Next to the skeleton, you see a series of hieroglyphs written on the coffin.

"I think these hieroglyphs tell how to open the coffin," your sister says. "That grave robber must have read them wrong."

Hieroglyphic writing can be read either forward or backward. The animal symbols always face the start of a sentence!

Draw the birds' heads facing right or left. Both birds should face the same way. When you're done, tear along the dotted line and fold over this flap.

LEFT **RIGHT**

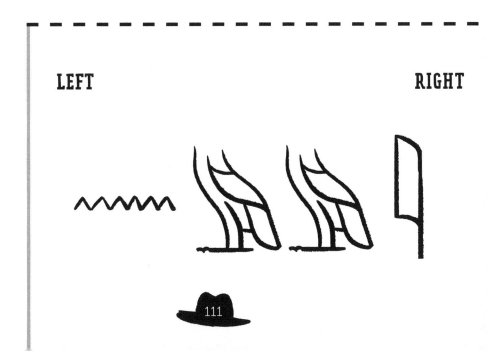

Aces!

"The hieroglyphs say that to unlock the coffin, we need to first write the name of the pharaoh who's in this tomb," your sister tells you. "It's a good thing the pharaoh shares your name!"

Ancient Egyptians believed that a dead person would "live again" if their name was spoken, so they were sure to put the pharaoh's name all over the tomb.

The English alphabet has 26 letters, but the ancient Egyptians invented a system of writing made up of 700 hieroglyphs, or pictures of animals and objects. Scribes did all the writing in ancient Egypt. They were chosen for the job as kids and trained for years to master the language.

You need to get good at it NOW! Go to the next page.

Are your birds facing to the right? Turn to page 158.

Are your birds facing to the right? Turn to page 158.

Birds looking to the left? Flip to the next page.

You can't match every letter from our alphabet to a hieroglyph. We have such different languages. The chart below shows a simplified version that translates to our alphabet. Use this chart to write your name in hieroglyphs on the line below.

a	b	c	d	e
f	g	h	i	j
k	l	m	n	o
p	q	r	s	t
u	v	w	x	y
z	ch	Kh	sh	

When you're done, turn to page 53.

"'Secret Image of Ha' is the name of my right foot," you say. "'Flower of Hathor' is the name of my left foot."

And the floor says, "You know us. You may pass."

Well done! You walk across the floor to the Hall of Truth. Here you'll be tested by 42 gods to see if you've been a good person!

Being kind was very important to the ancient Egyptians.

You think about how you laughed at Ineni and hurt her feelings this morning—um, you hope the gods won't ask about that!

Besides, you think, you've been *pretty* good, especially when compared to other pharaohs in history. For example, the pharaoh Pepi II ordered that his servants be covered with honey—that way, swarming flies would land on them and not him!

Whoa, and some people think I'm tough!

Draw a picture of Pepi II and his servants so you can show the gods.

114

When you're finished, go to page 56.

"Come on," you say. "We have to get back to the surface and find Mom."

You give Chione a boost into the star shaft next to the first head, and the two of you scurry up the steep passage. It's not easy going, and it only gets harder as you climb higher.

Your foot comes down on a loose stone, which is actually a trigger. It sets off a booby trap! A huge boulder drops into the shaft over your heads and starts rolling toward you.

Remember the beginning of this adventure, when you escaped being flattened by the boulder? I'm afraid you won't be so lucky this time.

Good thing you like pancakes!

END

That's just a flat-out sad ending. Let's get a redo on page 147.

You wake up with a jolt! Your head falls back on a stone pillow. When you tear off the blindfold and look around, you gasp. You're in a torch-lit burial chamber!

Hmm. I know it's probably part of the game. But this is ancient Egypt—you might want to make sure you're not a mummy.

I got a little woozy thinking about mummies. Can you finish three of the drawings for me?

6 STEPS TO MAKING A MUMMY IN 70 DAYS

Draw the brain here. Ick!

Draw the lungs in the jar.

1. Priests use a hook to pull out the brain through the nose—and throw it away. They believe the heart is the source of intelligence.

2. Other organs are dried out and put into containers called canopic jars.

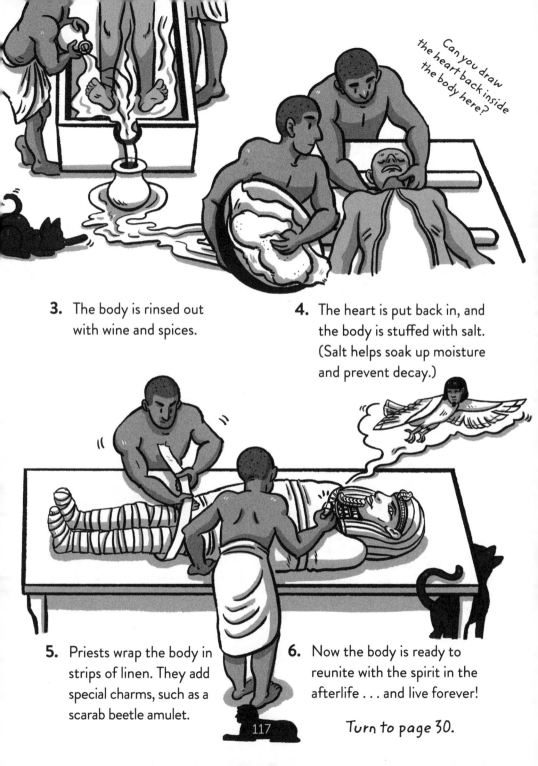

Can you draw the heart back inside the body here?

3. The body is rinsed out with wine and spices.

4. The heart is put back in, and the body is stuffed with salt. (Salt helps soak up moisture and prevent decay.)

5. Priests wrap the body in strips of linen. They add special charms, such as a scarab beetle amulet.

6. Now the body is ready to reunite with the spirit in the afterlife . . . and live forever!

Turn to page 30.

You remember that the pyramid worker's hint talked about a stomachache, so you tap the door behind the pig teeth. A hollow *thunk* tells you this could be the door you need!

There's one way to find out. You push on it, and the wood slides back. A dark, narrow passage is revealed.

"Quick!" you say to your sister. You both dart inside and close the door behind you just as you hear Dr. Venison and James coming out of the burial chamber.

You and Chione scurry along the passage. It suddenly splits into two shafts that slope almost straight up. You think you could make the steep climb up either one.

"I know what these shafts are!" Chione says.

PAGE
177

Draw what an ancient Egyptian might have looked for at the top of these shafts.

Did your drawing include the sun? Flip to page 124.

118

Does your view show lots of stars? Go to page 146.

"Leave the priceless artifact that is probably the most important discovery of this century!" you shout as you take your sister's hand and pull her into the inky darkness.

Well, you might as well have shouted it.
I can't believe you left a piece of that boat behind!

I'm not the only one who's enraged. As you run through the night, unable to see where you're going, one of those cranky hippos appears right in front of you.

Sprinting at full speed, you collide face-first with the animal. Its cranky factor multiplies by 100.

Have you ever seen a steamroller flatten an orange?

I think I might have just seen something very similar.

END

Ugh! I can't look! Return to page 164!

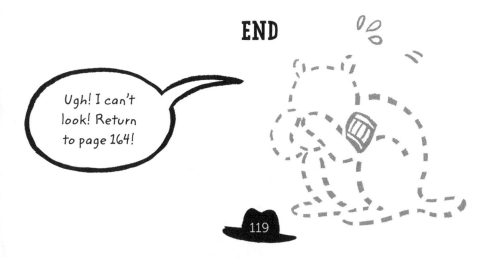

"You know, the Great Pyramid will have about two million three hundred thousand stone blocks," you say to Den and the rest of the crew. "That means we only need to push about two million more!"

But no one laughs at your joke—because no one is listening. You're all alone. Where'd everybody go?

You peek over the edge of the level you're on. Down below you see the vizier and his guards dragging away your crew!

Oh no! Are you in trouble for writing on the stone? Have you defiled the holy structure somehow? But workers do it all the time. This doesn't seem fair!

"Wait!" you shout, and Den hears you. He looks up, confused and scared, but is pulled away before he can say anything.

And you know why he looks worried. Punishment for a minor crime could involve cutting off the person's nose! In fact, one pharaoh created a city of the noseless for all the people he punished.

City of the Noseless

Give the citizens of this city their schnozzes back!
Draw noses on all the people and animals. Then turn to page 148.

You and your sister scramble up the shaft. Yes! You chose the correct way out! The shaft opens to the outside of the pyramid. Carefully, you climb onto the sloping pyramid wall and look up. You're still underground, but you can see faint moonlight coming through the hole you and Chione fell through.

"Let's get to the top of the pyramid," you say. "Hopefully we can climb out of the hole from there."

"Stop!" James shouts from below. He and Dr. Venison are scampering up the star shaft toward you.

Go! Go! Go!

Once at the very tip of the pyramid, you find you can't reach the hole after all. You'll have to knock your way out. You and Chione start pounding on the plaster ceiling. At first nothing happens. But then it starts to crack....

The ancient Egyptians didn't have sunglasses—and staring at the sun would hurt anyone's eyes, including yours! In fact, you're rubbing your own as the Venisons catch up to you!

END

You can still be the star of this story. Go back to page 118 and try again!

Rush to page 164!

124

Good job! You decide to leave another message for the pharaoh in the empty coffin and one more inside the pyramid's entrance. The second message tells him to check out the burial chamber closely.

As you finish the last message, you hear a loud voice: "You there! Stop!"

It's the vizier. He's about 200 yards away, pointing you out to the guards with him. They start running toward you.

Time for you to flee! Choose one of these ways to escape!

Feet: Most people get around on foot, wearing sandals made of papyrus. You already have a pair of feet attached to your body, but those soldiers are FAST!

Chariot: This horse-drawn vehicle with two wheels is used in war and races. *Go to page 157.*

Litter: This human-powered transport is basically a platform. You'll need four people to hold the poles as you ride in style in the middle. *Flip to page 110.*

Donkey: A lot of people ride these animals, but just like your donkey, this one looks way too slow to make a big escape.

Boat: A sailboat can go super fast on the Nile—up to 124 miles per day. But you can't get to your family in the desert by boat!

YES! You did it!

With a little push on the side of the boat, you and your sister step aboard—

Just then James and Dr. Venison burst out of the darkness and race toward the riverbank as if they're about to jump in and swim after you.

"I wouldn't do that if I were you!" your sister shouts.

"Why not?" James asks with a sneer.

"Um, 'cause there's a hungry crocodile in the water!" you yell. But you're not a very good liar.

"Your bluffing won't stop us!" Dr. Venison says.

"Well, then we will!" you hear someone shout.

It's your mom! And she has a four-person security team with her. They immediately grab the Venisons.

"Kids!" your mom says. "I'm so glad we found you! I had a feeling these two were up to no good, and I see I was right!"

"And that's not the only thing you were right about, Mom!" Chione calls.

You look down. Yes, you made your escape, but you also proved that your mom has been correct all along.

The ancient solar boat floats!

It's time to celebrate! Turn to page 74.

PYRAMID WORKER PATH

Well, you've certainly picked a tough row to hoe!

In more ways than one. . . . See what I mean, below.

Until last year, when you began working on the pyramid, you and your family plowed your farm by hand.

1. Hold your pen or pencil between two fingers, like this.

2. Now see if you can hoe three straight rows for your crops on page 129, going from START to FINISH while avoiding all the obstacles.

3. Start over if you hit a rock, an animal, or another obstacle in the field.

I've done one row for you. Not so easy, is it?
Hoe three rows for your crops.

FINISH

START

Well done! Before you turn the page, write an adjective (A)
and your favorite celebrity (B) in the blanks.

_____ A 🔺129 B _____

Every year the Nile River floods. You can't work in the fields when they're underwater. That's why many farmers (like you!) are required to work on big projects—such as pyramids—during the flood season.

Building a pyramid is HARD. You push tons of rock uphill. Broken bones and crushed limbs are dangers of life on a construction site. But in some ways, you like it. Now that you're working on the pyramid, you can afford a donkey to pull a plow for your family.

As you head off to work, you say goodbye to your donkey.

Write the word from the blanks on page 129 here.

↓

"See you later, _____   _____!"

A   B

130

Before you go, take a long look at your donkey.
Now close your eyes and draw the ears and tail.
Try again till your donkey can hear you and give you
a tail-swish goodbye. Then turn to page 20.

131

You read the message aloud: "'Find the key to your escape inside the coffin'!"

"That's great," Chione says. "But we have to get out and warn Mom that the pyramid is being raided by thieves!"

The worker's message might be just what it takes to make that happen. You need to find the coffin!

Wondering if this pyramid is like others you've studied, you think of the map of the Great Pyramid of Giza. It looks like this:

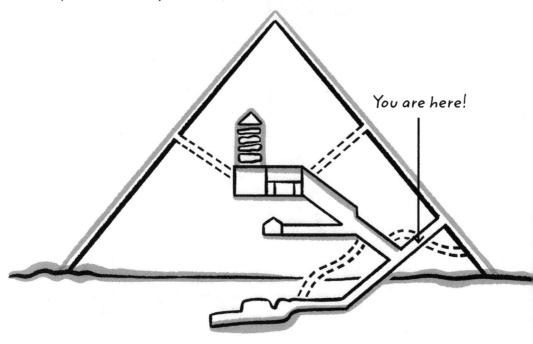

You are here!

The tunnel ahead splits in two directions—one up and one down. Which way should you go to find the coffin?

Hurry! I can hear Dr. Venison and James right behind you!

If you choose to go up, turn to page 81.
Want to go down? Turn to page 161.

"Don't worry, my child!" Mom says, seeing how anxious you look. "Your father is fine! He wanted me to tell you that he has a surprise for you!"

I can't wait to hear it. . . . Your dad has great surprises!

"He's busy setting up a royal game called Escape the Underworld, just for you. It's unlike any that Egypt—or the world—has ever seen. Your father says you can be pharaoh for a day if you can escape the game!"

Egyptians at this time believe the underworld is a big part of the afterlife. Here's a quick tour! Trace a path from START to FINISH in the maze. In the blanks below, write down the two numbers on your path. Then go to that page!

Turn to page _____ _____.

If you're having a tough time, go to page 183 for the answer.

The sun is already scorching hot when you reach the flooded Nile River and jump on the 35-foot-long barge that's waiting for you.

"Let's go!" you say. Eight men begin rowing, and the barge carries you quickly downstream (to the north). Boats traveling upstream use sails to catch the wind, while boats going downstream rely on oarsmen and the current.

On the barge is a giant block of sandstone that weighs 30 tons. It's from a nearby quarry, and you're in charge of getting it to the pyramid construction site.

Because Egyptians don't use nails, the boat makers use rope to tie pieces of wood together. They push reeds into the gaps to help prevent leaks. Trees in Egypt don't grow tall enough to make long planks, so most boats are a hodgepodge of smaller pieces.

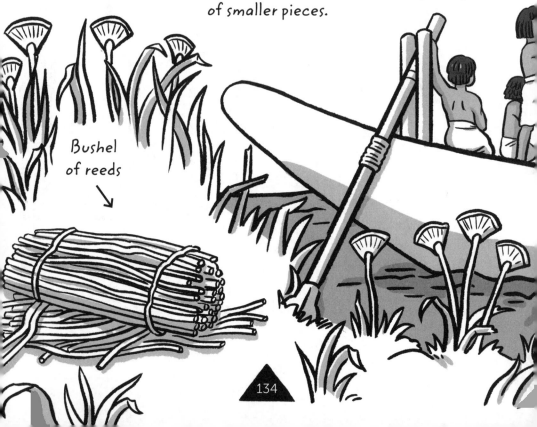

Bushel of reeds

Uh-oh. Your barge has sprung a leak in the front. Quick! Draw as many bushels of reeds as you can in the hole.

Did you draw two or more bushels? Fold down this flap.

If you drew one bushel, turn up this flap.

You fixed it! Turn to page 156.

Aces! You keep floating down the river. The block you're carrying might be one of thousands needed to build the massive pyramid, but each stone is important. You want the pyramid to be perfect for your friend and—

Wait a second. Take a gander at that fancy boat! A wealthy scribe is being rowed around by 18 oarsmen while musicians and a singer perform for him. See that smaller boat tied up to the big one? That's his kitchen boat, and his servants are about to make him lunch!

That's not ful-filling—your boat sinks.

What kind of ancient Egyptian boat would you want?
Draw it here.

Just curious: Did you draw a motor on your boat?

YES, turn to page 174.
NO, go to page 82.

"*Roar!*" a voice says from the shadows. Your blood runs cold, and you're about to take off.

Then you hear a giggle. "Sorry, did I scare you?"

It's your little sister! Chione is a year younger than you, but she's incredibly smart and really observant! She can tell when the slightest thing has changed.

Circle the differences in the pictures.
How many can you spot?
Write that number in the blank below.

Turn to page 8__.

If you can't get the answer, head to page 183.

"Hmm," you say. "It looks like the message is telling us to go back to the cat mummies!"

"Do you think the key to our escape is there?" Chione asks doubtfully.

"One way to find out," you say. The two of you sneak back to the mortuary with the thousands of cat mummies. The Venisons must still be looking for you on the lower level of the pyramid.

"The key could be here!" you say, reaching up to a mortuary wall with shelves that hold about 70 or 80 mummies.

SNICK! Whooosh! That's the sound of a wall cracking and scores of cat mummies falling through the air . . . right on top of you!

END

Me-OW! Go back to page 102 and try again!

Oh! I know the writer of Dead of the Book! She's a dear friend of mine. Her name is Yulenever Bea Faro. Say her name out loud and you'll understand why I don't think you'll like her as well as I do.

Your escape is over!

END

No, it's not! Write a new ending for yourself. Go back to page 31 and try again!

You hear your friends onshore laughing. Everyone in your work crew gets along, even though you're all very different. Egyptians believe in the value of finding a job for all people. Like other work crews, your group calls itself by a funny name: the No Eyebrows.

PAGE
177

Why? It's a show of support from your crew. You and your family plucked out your eyebrows when your cat died a few weeks ago. You'll mourn and be sad until your eyebrows grow back.

Den, your best friend from the crew, jumps into the water to join you. After you play and splash around together for a minute, you both climb out onto the bank. The rest of your team is teasing you by singing a popular song. To sing along, first fill in the words on this page.

That's Den!

PLUCK!

Write an example for each of the words below.

_____
verb

_____
adverb

_____
place

_____
person

_____
person

_____
color

_____
object

← *When you're done, fold over this flap.*

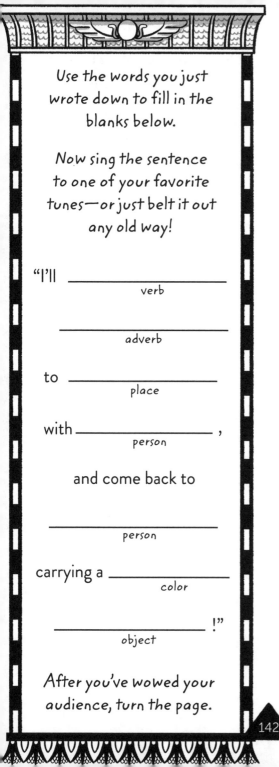

Use the words you just wrote down to fill in the blanks below.

Now sing the sentence to one of your favorite tunes—or just belt it out any old way!

"I'll _____
verb

_____
adverb

to _____
place

with _____ ,
person

and come back to

_____
person

carrying a _____
color

_____ !"
object

After you've wowed your audience, turn the page.

142

That's enough lollygagging about. The vizier would love to find a reason to fire you. Time to get back to work!

"All right," you tell your crew. "We need to get this stone block from the dock up onto that pyramid!"

The Egyptians haven't invented wheeled carts strong enough to carry it yet. Instead, you use smooth logs called sledges. Your team pushes and pulls the stone over them. Sledges are more slippery when they're wet. . . . Pour some water on yours first!

You reach the bottom of the half-done pyramid. How will you get the block—which weighs about as much as 20 adult hippopotamuses— up onto the construction site? It's way too heavy to lift.

PAGE 180

Maybe you build a ramp that wraps around the pyramid from bottom to top? After you push the stones onto the pyramid, you can just remove the ramp.

Go to the next page.

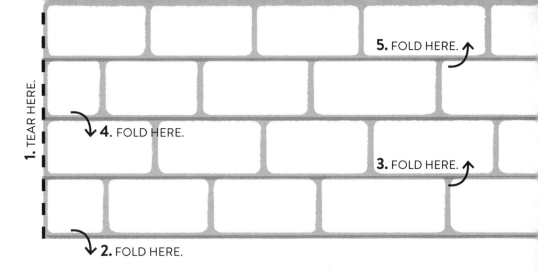

1. TEAR HERE.

5. FOLD HERE. ↗

4. FOLD HERE.

3. FOLD HERE. ↗

2. FOLD HERE.

BUILD YOUR OWN PYRAMID!

A. Follow the directions to tear along the vertical line. Then fold along each horizontal line in the direction of the arrows. You'll construct your own not-yet-finished pyramid.

B. Now impress your boss, the vizier, with your know-how. How many levels do you need to lift this stone to get it on top of your current pyramid?

Write that number in the blank below.

Turn to page 142 + _____.

Okay, okay. Here's a hint: After you make the folds in your pyramid, just count the steps from the ground up!

If you can't get the answer, turn to page 183.

Aces! You and the rest of the No Eyebrows got the stone in place! Crews are so proud of doing their job that they often leave their mark. You write your crew name in hieroglyphs on the wall of the pyramid—not too flashy or anything.

Show your pride! Use these number hieroglyphs to write the year you were born on the wall.

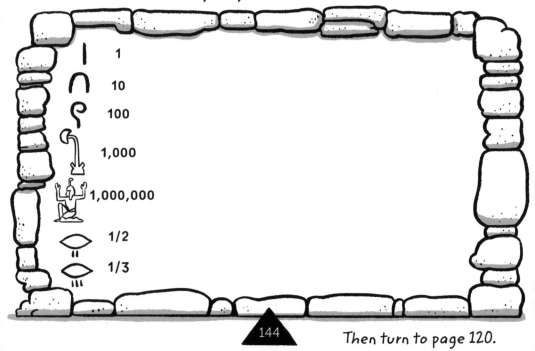

	1
	10
	100
	1,000
	1,000,000
	1/2
	1/3

144

Then turn to page 120.

Carrying your senet game, you sneak into the vizier's palace. You manage to slip past all his guards, and you find him in his garden . . . alone. When he sees you, he sneers, "You! What are you doing here?"

"I'm here to rescue my friends!" you announce bravely.

The vizier doesn't seem to know what you're talking about. Instead, he points to the game board. "I'll play senet with you," he says. "If I win, you stay away from the pharaoh forever. You will no longer be friends."

"And if I win?" you ask.

The vizier just shrugs. "We'll see. . . ."

Unfortunately, you do win. And the vizier is not a good sport! In fact, he might be the worst sport in all of ancient Egypt. As he calls the guards to have you hauled off to prison, you say a quick goodbye to the outside world.

END

Let's keep you out of jail! Return to page 148!

145

You drew stars—well done! That's what the ancient Egyptians might've looked for when they gazed up. Of course, you're underground . . . so you see only darkness above.

"It won't take the Venisons long to figure out where we are!" Chione says. "One of these two star shafts will lead us out of this chamber. But which one?"

You tap your chin thoughtfully. "I think the drawings of heads at the bottom of the shafts must be clues, right?" you ask.

"Yes!" Chione says. "One of them must belong to the mother from the clue! If we pick that head, we can escape!"

Go to the next page.

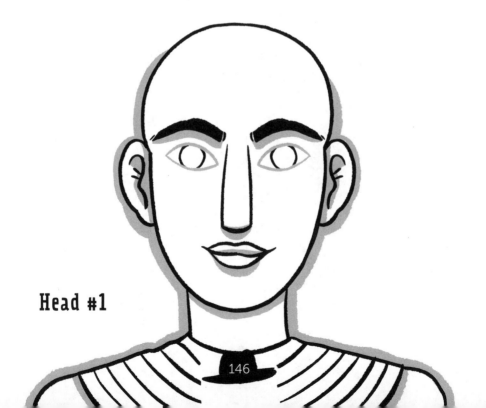

Head #1

146

I suppose I can help you. Follow these instructions:

- Add a false beard like this to Head #2:

- Give each face strong eyeliner.

- Place a wig like this on Head #2:

- Give both heads an earring.

- Draw this single braid on the right side of Head #1:

Which of the heads shows a mother?
Head #1? Turn to page 115.
Head #2? Go to page 122.

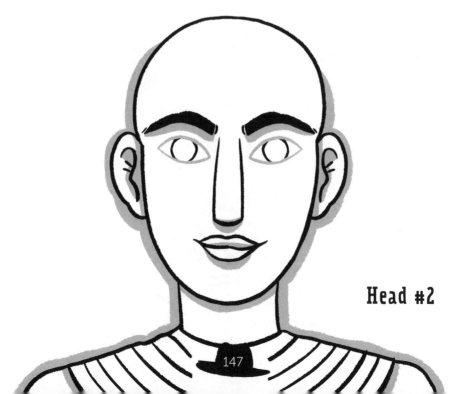

Head #2

147

It's true that the vizier doesn't want you to be friends with the pharaoh, but you can't believe how unfairly he's acting. You don't want your crew to get punished for something **you** did. You could admit to everything and take the blame before they get hurt.

But what about your family? If you're in trouble with the vizier, they could be, too.

What should you do?

If you run after the vizier and your crew, go to page 150.

If you race home to warn your family, turn to page 152.

Entomb?! Your stomach flip-flops.

Hundreds of years before you were born, early rulers, like King Djet, sacrificed their servants and mummified them. That way, the servants could wait on them in the afterlife. King Djet might have had as many as 580 mummified servants in his tomb. Is that what your friend the pharaoh wants to do to you and your crew?

If so, you might want to choose better friends!

Luckily, things in your time are much different! Shabti dolls have replaced actual people in tombs. Shabtis are small figurines that magically come alive in the afterlife and work in the fields and do other manual labor. Wealthy people fill their coffins and tombs with these dolls. That way they never have to lift a finger in the afterlife!

PAGE 178

Why would the pharaoh go back to the horrible old ways? There's one person who might have the answer!

If you go speak to the great ruler King Djet, turn to page 169.

Want to talk to the shabti doll maker? Flip to page 160.

You're going to help your friends escape from the vizier by taking the blame. Why not sweeten his mood? You made a board game called senet for your brother, but you decide to give it to the vizier. Take it for a test drive to make sure it works.

HOW TO PLAY A QUICK GAME:

1. Place your playing piece in the lower right space, and put one for a second player (real or imaginary) in the upper left space.

2. Take turns flipping a coin: heads move three spaces; tails, move four.

3. You can move in any direction, but you can't land on a space that is occupied by an object or another player.

4. The first player to reach the other's starting point wins.

**PLAYER #2
STARTS HERE**

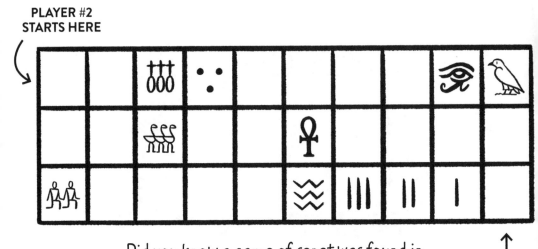

Did you know a game of senet was found in King Tut's tomb? It's an early version of backgammon, but no one is totally sure of the rules!

↑
**YOU
START
HERE**

Once you've played a couple of times, turn to page 145.

Papyrus is way too expensive for your family. So your brother wrote a message on bits of broken pottery.

Few Egyptians know how to read. But because of your new job, you and your brother have learned. Still, he messes up sometimes. Unscramble the mixed-up boldfaced words below so that the message makes sense.

We do **tno** __ __ __ understand what's

ggnoi __ __ __ __ __ on, but to be safe

we **twen** __ __ __ __ to our favorite spot

in **hte** __ __ __ desert. Join us!

Why does the vizier want to entomb you?

Love, Your Brother

The double-underlined letters spell out where to go next!

Turn to page one hundred forty- __ __ __ __.

Are you stuck?
Head to page
183 for the
answer.

You took a wrong turn. Try again!

151

Aces! Go to page 154.

You sprint back to the village. The streets have never felt so narrow—you could reach out and touch the houses on either side.

You're lucky you're too distracted to notice the smell. For toilets, people use boxes of sand underneath seats. Add that to the animal waste everywhere, and this village reeks!

Run through the maze below. Watch your step! When you finish, tear on the dotted lines and lift the flap you land on.

START

**FINISH 1**

152

FINISH 2

Um, something's gone very, very wrong. Take a look around. Need I say more?

END

Let's not **draw out** this bad ending. Return to page 18 and try another sketch on for size!

When you get close to your house, you run into a neighbor, who tells you, "Your family went out to the desert to bury your cat."

That surprises you. The cat burial was supposed to take place tomorrow. Why would your family leave early?

You continue on to your house. Inside, it takes only a second to see that your family is really gone. The large room is empty except for two stools, a box, a few storage jars, and the floor mats you sleep on. Shrines to ancestors and a few sculptures of gods sit on shelves.

Of course, nothing is made of wood. That's too rare.

I think your brother might have left you a note. Do you see any pieces of broken pottery?

Write the numbers of the broken pottery pieces where they belong on these jars. Turn to the page number you see.

Stuck? Head to page 183 for the answer!

You're not sure whose side the shabti maker is on. Carefully you ask, "Do you know about the vizier's plan for the pharaoh's tomb?"

The man nods and says, "But I won't have time to make the dolls. It's much easier to have you and the others mummified."

"That's his p-plan?" you stammer. You're not interested in having your brain pulled out through your nose and being turned into a mummy!

"You mean you didn't know?" the man asks.

"I can't believe the pharaoh would do a thing like this," you say.

"Oh, the pharaoh doesn't know about it. It's all the vizier's idea."

The pharaoh isn't aware of this evil plan! You need to warn your friend—if you're not already too late.

"Wait! Wait!" the man calls as you race out of the workshop.

But you keep running. Your first instinct is to go to the pharaoh's palace, but you'll never get past the guards. Where else might the pharaoh go? Where could he be?

*To brainstorm, draw your favorite place
here. Then turn to page 18.*

Nice choice! You have two chariots to pick from.

Do you jump on the first one and take off? Go to page 166.

Or do you take the time to break the other chariot so no one can chase you? Tear along the dotted lines, fold over the flap, and read the back!

"On ho!" Chione says. Wait. What did she say?

"Tahw?" you ask. Hold on. What on earth did you say?

"Gnorw ti did ew," she tells you.

Oh, I get it! You must have written the hieroglyph facing in the wrong direction. Now everything is backward!

While you and your sister try to figure out what's happening, the Venisons burst into the chamber. "Uoy evah ew won!" they shout at the same time.

DNE

You took too long, and the vizier's guards grabbed you!

END

Try again!

Let's turn everything back around! Try again on page 111.

Uh-oh. I thought I mentioned that cats were considered godlike in ancient Egypt.

And you **trapped** one? Maybe that's why a stone slab falls in the doorway of the burial chamber, blocking any possible chance of escape. Ever.

Now who's trapped?

END

PURR
PURR
PURR

I'm **feline** like I want a happier ending! Go back to page 73!

Sticking to the shadows as much as possible, you run to the shabti maker's workshop.

You look at the rows of dolls he's working on. Each one has a spell inscribed on it. When the dead person says the spells, the figures will come to life. A few of them carry tiny tools that they'll use for eternity.

What kind of shabti would you make? Draw it here.
Be sure to give it the clothes and tools it will need
to work in the afterlife!

HELP WANTED

FOR THE AFTERLIFE

Finished? Go to page 156!

You take your sister's hand and pull her along behind as you race down the passage. After all, burial chambers are "buried"—they should be down in the ground, right?

Wrong.

In this case, anyway . . . and this is the only case that matters.

"We've got them trapped!" you hear Dr. Venison tell his son.

They're right behind you, and I'm afraid there's no other way out.

END

I know a way out of this mess! Turn back to page 132!

Your mind is still racing. What news about your dad could possibly be so serious?

He was fine yesterday when he took you and your friends to a pretend hunt. He ordered his servants to make targets that looked like monsters, and you threw spears at them. Just like you, your dad loves games—the bigger the better!

Maybe one of the spears accidentally hit your dad? As you try to remember, you trace the path of each spear.

I've done one path for you. Why? Because I'm wonderful!

If a spear hit your dad, turn to page 23.

If all the spears missed your dad, go to page 133.

You're free! Now you need to get back to your mom at the campsite.

Do you take the time to grab the piece
of the boat you dug up? Turn to page 107.

Or do you just run into the night? Go to page 119.

I'm sorry, I think I have something in my eye. It's either a piece of dust or . . . wait, maybe it's REALITY!

Ancient Egyptians believed that if you drew something correctly, it might become a reality.

That's a pretty unhappy ending!

END

I like your imagination, my friend! *Go-pher* it again on page 80.

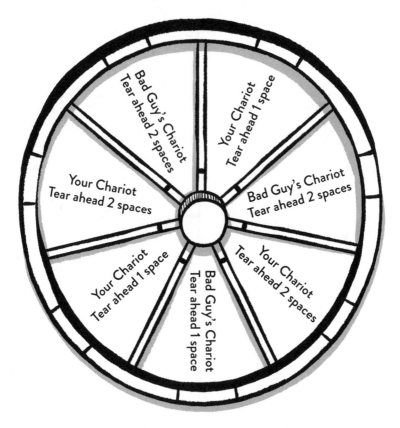

This is why I love being an escapologist!
This will be a chariot chase that you'll never forget!

One of the vizier's guards hops onto the other chariot and chases after you.
If you're not very fast (and very lucky!), he'll catch you. Go, go!

Here's what you do:

1. Play this game alone. Close your eyes, twirl your finger over the wheel above, and count to three. On three, bring your finger down and follow the directions on the space closest to your finger. For example, if it says *Your Chariot: Tear ahead 2 spaces*, tear along the dotted line to the left of *YOUR CHARIOT* up two spaces, fold up the flap, and read the text on the back.

2. The first chariot to the top wins!

BAD GUY'S CHARIOT

YOUR CHARIOT

You did it! Turn to page 170!

Did the bad guy get here first? Unfold and flatten both strips and start over!

So close!

The bad guy is on the move!

You can do it!

The bad guy is fast!

Keep going!

Watch out for the bad guy.

You're off to a good start.

Uh-oh! Here comes the bad guy!

YOUR CHARIOT

BAD GUY'S CHARIOT

You increase your
lead as the guard
gets covered in
sand! Turn to
page 172.

Balloons haven't
been invented yet!
Try again.

You sneak into King Djet's resting place. But guards must have seen you! They rush into the chamber and grab you just as you open his . . . coffin. That's all right. You were going to have a pretty one-sided conversation with the king anyway.

Don't you remember?
I told you King Djet died hundreds of years ago!

END

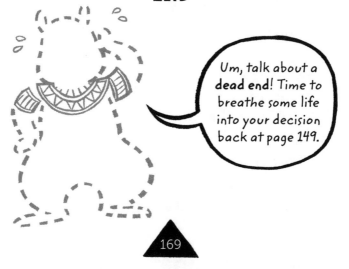

Um, talk about a
dead end! Time to
breathe some life
into your decision
back at page 149.

Excellent! You've pulled ahead, but you're still being chased.

Did you know archers love chariots? They can tie the reins around their waists and have their hands free to shoot arrows. And that's just what the vizier's guard is getting ready to do.

You need to slow him down!

Draw an arrow to knock down one of the objects above. Choose wisely! Tear and fold down the flap of your target.

Trying to make a clean getaway? Sorry. Shampoo doesn't stop the bad guy. Try again!

The water splashes out and instantly soaks into the dry ground. Try again.

Aces! Racing way ahead of the other chariot, you ride out to the desert to find your family. After about 15 minutes, you spot them. Seconds later, you jump off the chariot and hug your brother and parents.

"Where have you been?" a voice demands from behind them.

It's your best friend, Den. He's safe after all! You're so relieved. You give him a hug, too, and then ask, "What happened to you?"

"It's a long story," Den says with a smile. "But the pharaoh saw the warning you left for him at the pyramid. He's really grateful! In fact, he's giving our whole crew a huge raise and better jobs! We can go back to work tomorrow!"

Yes! You pump your hands in the air. Your escape has really paid off!

Go to the next page.

Draw yourself jumping up and down
happily with your family and Den.

When you're done, turn to page 74.

Your speedboat looks amazing . . . at the bottom of the river. The first motor-boat won't be invented until around 1886, a couple thousand years in the future. As it is, your boat made of reeds sinks under the weight of the motor!

END

Let's get this boat afloat! Motor back to page 137 and give it another go.

ESCAPOLOGIST FILES

It turns out that this inscription never existed!
All the "mysterious" deaths could easily be explained.
Newspapers ran the story to get more people to buy copies.

Welcome to the Seven Wonders of the World Website!

Pyramids of Giza: oldest and only surviving site on the list

- Hanging Gardens of Babylon: described as having beautifully landscaped terraces
- Statue of Zeus at Olympia: giant sculpture of the god on a throne
- Temple of Artemis at Ephesus: huge building with ornate decoration
- Colossus of Rhodes: mega-sized statue built at a harbor
- Pharos of Alexandria: one of the most famous lighthouses in history
- Mausoleum of Halicarnassus: impressive tomb built for an ancient king

PHARAOH FASHIONS MAGAZINE

Want to look your best as THE pharaoh to watch this season? Don't forget your crook (the symbol of kingship) and your flail (the symbol of the land's fertility)! And never be caught without your crown! It's like two crowns in one—one part for Upper Egypt and the other for Lower Egypt.

Mummy Master Coach: Tip #55

The goal of being turned into a mummy is eternity in the afterlife. But to reach the afterlife, you first have to travel through the dangerous challenges of the underworld!

Hang in There!

Catlike creatures have been known to drive away Apep.

EGYPTIAN GODS DICTIONARY

HA: god of the Western Desert
HATHOR: goddess of delights, such as dance

Help Wanted: Can You Dig It?

The Museum of Ancient Magic wants to hire an archaeologist. If you "dig" studying past cultures by examining physical objects they left behind . . . this job could be for you!

Chariot and Driver Magazine
Ready, Set . . . Tut!

Even though they're thousands of years old, the six chariots found in King Tut's tomb are remarkably well preserved!

Big News from the Year 1954

Archaeologists have found a boat broken up into five sections buried next to the Great Pyramid. The pharaoh planned to sail across the sky with the sun god in the afterlife. Many believe that the 143-foot-long boat might actually float on water if reassembled today!

A Tomb with a View?

Some researchers think that shafts in pyramids might have been used by ancient astronomers to study and map constellations.

Best Friends FOREVER!

Pyramid builders worked together for years and could become great friends. They'd give their crews names like Pure Ones of Khufu. (Khufu was a pharaoh.) Archaeologists have found names that crews painted on pyramid blocks thousands of years ago.

VERY IMPORTANT!

Ancient Egyptians believed bad deeds would weigh down their hearts. A good person's heart was said to be lighter than a feather!

EGYPT THROUGH THE AGES

Parents in ancient Egypt loved their kids. When they could, Mom and Dad showered them with toys, games . . . and exotic pets, like colorful birds and baboons. Sports and fun activities filled childhood—which was pretty short!

AGE

5 Boys and girls began working for their parents or started school.

14 Girls got married; boys married when older.

40 Egyptians in ancient times weren't likely to live past this age.

100 King Pepi II, who had the longest reign in Egypt, may have reached this ripe old age!

Ask the Super Sphinx-er

Dear Super Sphinx-er,
When I get to the afterlife, I don't want to lift a finger. What should I do?
Dunno Pharaoh

Dear Dunno Pharaoh,
I have one word for you: shabti! Get yourself as many shabti dolls as you can. They'll come to life in the afterlife and do all the work for you. Otherwise, you could try to "convince" 580 servants to drink poison, like King Djet probably did. Good luck!

The Super Sphinx-er

BE ART SMART!

Egyptian rulers appear to be fit and healthy in ancient drawings, but that wasn't always true. Thanks in part to tasty sugary treats like honey and dried fruit, some pharaohs, such as Hatshepsut, were probably overweight and might have suffered from diabetes. King Tut had a bad foot and a curved spine, and he might have walked with a cane.

WALK-IN LIKE AN EGYPTIAN!

"When I get sick in the ancient world, Egypt is the place to go!" says Gori, 14, from ancient Rome. "The clinics there are the best. The healers might cover you with crocodile droppings, but it's totally worth it to get rid of pesky demons!"

TOMB TRAPPER 2.5

Our latest **TOMB TRAPPER** is based on the ancient Egyptian model that nabbed a would-be robber in 1944. He reached into a coffin to grab some treasure, and the lid fell and trapped him. Then the roof collapsed on top of him!

Halloween Happenings Magazine

Your Look Checklist!

Want to look the part at your next costume party? Here's who wore what back in ancient Egypt!

	Men	Women
Makeup	X	X
Single braid	X	
Fake beard	X	X
Wigs after plucking hair	X	X

Queen Hatshepsut can be seen wearing a false beard in drawings—it was a sign of power!

COUNT-THE-CATS CONTEST!

Want to win a couple hundred thousand cat mummies? Now's your chance! About 130 years ago, an Egyptian farmer discovered a mass burial site while digging in the sand. He uncovered hundreds of thousands of mummified cats from around 1000 BCE! Some were sold to tourists, and many were sold as fertilizer. In fact, 180,000 were spread in England to help crops grow. Can you guess the number of cat mummies the farmer found? Mail your guess to

---

Sadly, slavery did exist in ancient Egypt, and enslaved people worked in fields and homes. But they did not build the great pyramids of Egypt, as many once thought. Pyramid workers were farmers and other free Egyptians who had to devote a few months of the year to the pharaohs' grand projects.

RAMPS R US

While you're building your pyramid, have you noticed that dragging a stone block straight up is way too much work? We bet you have! Why not let us build you a temporary ramp around the site? You can pull the block up and around on a much more gentle slope. And when you're done, simply take away the ramp. These are just two possible ramp models we offer!

MODEL A   MODEL B

ADDITIONAL EXPLORING

Here are a few of the books that the Master Escapologist
used for research when putting together this adventure.

Blair, Beth L., and Jennifer A. Ericsson. *The Everything Kids'
Mummies, Pharaohs, and Pyramids Puzzle and Activity Book.*
New York: Simon & Schuster, 2008.

Boyer, Crispin. *Everything Ancient Egypt.* Washington, D.C.:
National Geographic Kids, 2012.

Galford, Ellen. *Hatshepsut: The Girl Who Became a Great Pharaoh.*
Washington, D.C.: National Geographic Kids, 2007.

Hart, George. *Eyewitness: Ancient Egypt.* New York: DK, 2014.

Manley, Bill. *The Penguin Historical Atlas of Ancient Egypt.*
New York: Penguin Books, 1996.

Mann, Elizabeth. *The Great Pyramid.* New York: Mikaya Press, 1996.

Mertz, Barbara. *Red Land, Black Land.* New York: William Morrow, 2009.

Morley, Jacqueline. *You Wouldn't Want to Be a Pyramid Builder! A Hazardous
Job You'd Rather Not Have.* Rev. ed. New York: Scholastic, 2014.

Putnam, James. *Eyewitness: Mummy.* New York: DK, 2009.

Sands, Emily. *The Egyptology Handbook: A Course in the Wonders of Egypt.*
Somerville, MA: Candlewick Press, 2005.

Sloan, Christopher. *Mummies: Dried, Tanned, Sealed, Drained, Frozen,
Embalmed, Stuffed, Wrapped, and Smoked . . . and We're Dead Serious.*
Washington, D.C.: National Geographic Kids, 2010.

Spencer, Neal. *Book of Egyptian Hieroglyphs.*
New York: Barnes and Noble, 2003.

ANSWERS

p. 23:

p. 41: The spell is: "May you walk on your feet; may you not walk upside down."

p. 53: The rebus solution is: The doctor's stomachache fix is a door to the true mother star.

p. 65: Go back to page 16.

p. 73: Starting with the marble at the top of the chute, the path is as follows: The marble rolls down the stairs and hits the dominos, which tips the cup of water. The water fills the bowl, which tilts the plank and makes the boot hit the ball that's waiting on the step. The ball rolls until it hits the hamster wheel, causing the hamster to run, which moves the belt. The belt pulls the hand down, which strikes the match and lights the candle. The flame burns the string. When the string is broken, the weight drops on the balloon, which forces the air out and blows the knife over. The knife cuts the string, and the cage falls over the mouse.

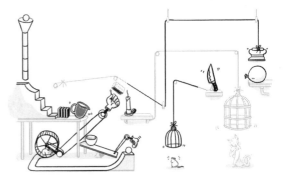

p. 79:

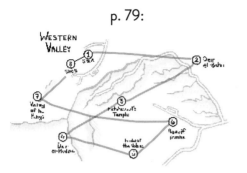

p. 83:

p. 95:

p. 93: Turn to page 95.

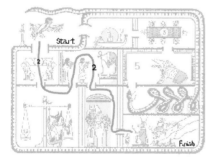

p. 99: There are three look-alike cat mummies, which means you should turn to page 100.

p. 102: The rebus solution is: Find the key to your escape inside the coffin.

p. 133: The correct answer is 22.

p. 138: Turn to page 84.

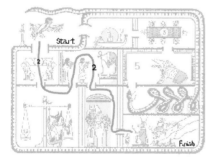

p. 143: Turn to page 144 (142 + 2).

p. 151: Turn to page one hundred forty-nine.

p. 155: Turn to page 151.

Congratulations!

You have proven yourself worthy, and you're one step closer to becoming my assistant . . . and perhaps someday a Master Escapologist.

Now, as promised, I will reveal more about myself.

To unlock my note, you need to find a pyramid on something you use all the time. (I'm talking about a one-dollar bill.)

What's at the top of the pyramid on that everyday thing? It's the key to reading my message to you.

Right now [[?]] am a prisoner! [[?]] am locked [[?]]ns[[?]]de the only cell that has ever been able to hold me. But hopefully not for long . . . [[?]]f my books can tra[[?]]n you to help me.

Keep your escapes great (like mine), and someday we will meet!

Evolo Cherishwise,
Master Escapologist